I0739351

Aiki Flinthart

80AD
The Jewel of Asgard

(Book 1)

Aiki Flinthart

ISBN-13: 978-0-9945660-4-1
Computing Advantages & Training P/L

Discover other titles by Aiki Flinthart at:
www.aikiflinthart.com

Cover Art by : Jason Seabaugh

Review:
"This story is very unique. The premise is immensely entertaining. It's a great story!".......Chilli Tween Reads October 31st 2011

NOTE: this series is written with the young adult agegroup in mind. Having said that, thousands of adults have read and enjoyed them as well. Please bear this in mind when reading and leaving feedback.

80AD

Level One

The Jewel of Asgard.

LONG BAIYU

Cold held the chamber in its bitter grasp: an intense, unrelenting chill that soaked through skin and muscle and invaded aching bones. Bound in icy darkness, surrounded by stone and shadow, Long Baiyu crouched in a corner of his miserable cell and waited. What choice did he have? This place sucked warmth and hope from him, until all he could do was hurt and wait.

Sharp footsteps sounded outside his door. The heavy wood flew open. Long Baiyu raised an arm to shield his eyes from the overbright candle carried by his visitor. It had been too long since he'd seen the sun. He was weakened by darkness; too drained to even attempt an escape.

"Have you changed your mind?" his visitor demanded. The man was tall and arrogant with high, sharp cheekbones and narrow, dark eyes. He held heavy silken robes off the stone floor in visible disgust and looked down his long nose at the prisoner. Thin hands, blackened by chemical stains, raised the candle as he peered at his wretched hostage.

"Have you?" With an impatient sneer, he added, "If not, then you can continue rot down here. I don't care. I'll take what I need without your help. I only offer you the chance to live out of respect for our former friendship."

"Respect?" His captive smiled regretfully, his words a mere, painful whisper. "You show no respect for anyone – not even yourself. Look what you have become. You intend to use me for your own ends. Release me before your treachery is discovered and you may avoid the wrath of the Emperor. If I die here the Emperor will have you executed and you will never join your ancestors with honour."

The man laughed softly. "Your threats are empty. The boy-Emperor is in Luoyang. He's no obstacle to me and I don't intend to join my ancestors. I intend to live forever - unlike you, my old friend."

The menace in his voice sent a shiver down Baiyu's spine. But Baiyu shook his head.

"When the mantis hunts the locust, he forgets the shrike that is hunting him."

His captor raised a scornful eyebrow. "Don't give me that wiseman rubbish. You forget how long I've known you." When it was obvious Baiyu intended to say no more, his captor laughed again and left.

In darkness once more, Baiyu pulled in what little remaining strength he possessed and called on the power of the Ancestors. He had to escape – yet he could not do it alone. Around him, a faint purple-blue glow glimmered. Picking up a small, round pebble from underfoot, he held it in his narrow hand and blew gently on it twice. In a singsong voice, he chanted nonsense words over and over above the stone. Slowly, the light around him gathered into a thin, white-purple streak of lighting. It zipped around his head until he spoke to it sternly. Then it hovered above the stone for a second before spearing straight into it.

Baiyu whispered, trembling with the effort. The stone split neatly in two in his hand. Each half then twisted and merged back together before pulling apart again. The glow dimmed and Baiyu smiled in weary satisfaction. He raised his hand and blew again, murmuring more words of power.

Lifting his hand higher, he drew on everything he had left and whispered,

"Bring those that can free me."

The glow and the stone vanished with a crack! Plunged back into night, Long Baiyu collapsed.

****

CHAPTER ONE

PHOENIX

Phoenix glanced at his watch and groaned. Five-thirty. Late. Rising up on the bike pedals, he pushed harder, speeding down the sleepy suburban street. Driveways and front yards flashed past. Neighbours hallooed. He ignored them. If he was late again and Jacob found out…

He pedalled harder.

His driveway appeared. He slammed on the brakes, turning to slide into it with a spray of gravel. The adrenalin rush brought a smile of fierce joy to his face. A few more quick pushes brought him up the slight incline and around the back of the mansion he now called home. Well, the house where he lived, anyway. Peering into the garage, he heaved a sigh of relief. His mother wasn't home and neither was Jacob.

Leaning his bike against the house, Phoenix pulled out a key and let himself in through the kitchen door. He listened hard. The big, cold house was echoingly empty. Some of the tension went out of his shoulders. He dropped his aikido bag on the kitchen floor before slouching over to the fridge to inspect its contents. Since turning thirteen, six months before, he always seemed to be hungry. His mother teased him about it and, unfortunately, it also gave Jacob another reason to be annoyed with him.

After staring vaguely into the full fridge for a while, Phoenix grabbed container of cold pizza from dinner the night before. He shut the door then opened it again and picked out a can of Coke.

Car tyres crunched up the drive. Startled, he stared

over his shoulder at the back wall of the house, trying to work out whose car it was by sound. The distinctive thrum of a big engine, made him bolt for the stairs. Then he skidded to a stop. A car door slammed. Swearing under his breath, Phoenix dashed back and snatched up his aikido bag, shoving the pizza and drink into it as he turned again for the stairs. Seven long jumps brought him safely to the top where he stopped, leaning against a wall around the corner to catch his breath.

The kitchen door opened. Heavy footsteps rapped sharply across marble tiles. Phoenix didn't wait any longer. Jacob was home.

Stepping softly along the pile-carpeted hallway, he reached his own room, eased the door open, let himself in and closed it again; carefully. Only once it was closed did he lower the bag to the floor and finally breathe out. Dropping into the chair in front of his study desk, he opened the drink, sucked up the bubbles and switched on his computer.

Phoenix ran stiff fingers through his unruly mop of brown hair, and swivelled to stare out the window. Now, if he just kept his head low for an hour or so, his mother would come home and he could avoid a run-in with his stepfather. Jacob would know Phoenix was home by the fact his bike was there but they had an unspoken agreement to avoid each other whenever humanly possible. The only time they crossed paths was at dinner and Jacob Smithson never made any sort of fuss about his stepson in front of Gwen.

As Phoenix waited for his computer to boot up, he munched on pizza and thought about his life. There wasn't much to think about. Time passed; things happened all around him but he didn't actually feel a part of it. The endless round of school days just didn't seem real. He felt stuck, waiting for something to happen; for some miracle to make it like it used to be when Dad was alive. He snorted.

Like that was ever going to happen.

He had a couple of friends at school but no best buddies. His dad had always been his best friend and he just didn't feel like putting in the effort to make another. School itself was mindnumbingly boring - except for sports. He was good at sports but nowadays he didn't even get to do much of that. Every time he tried to stand up for himself and argue with Jacob over some dumb new rule, his stepfather punished him by cutting back on his outside school activities. The only stuff he got to do now was play computer games and go to aikido. Games were just a time-waster; an escape; a place to hide and not have to think. The dojo existed as the only place he felt alive. His Sensei was pretty much the only person who listened and understood, anyway.

Phoenix frowned. That was why he had to be home on time today: the threat from Jacob to pull him out of classes if he was late home again. He wasn't sure what he'd do if that happened. Run away?

His lips twisted into a scornful smile. Where to? He had nowhere to go. He wasn't old enough to earn a living and he'd seen what happened to other kids who ended up on the streets – drugs and whatever. Nah. He shook his head and began to check his messages. Jacob might be a prat but living in the same house with him remained better than the alternatives.

Besides, his mother was happy, and that was the most important thing. Phoenix all too clearly remembered hearing her cry herself to sleep every night for months after the car accident three years ago. He remembered the helpless anger; remembered how lost he'd felt and how frightened; how much he'd hoped his dad would just walk back in the house and say it had all been a big mistake. He still sometimes hoped that but he'd learned to live with it now. Honestly, he'd been glad when his mother had hooked up with Jacob. She'd stopped crying and started smiling again, at least.

OK, so Jacob wasn't an ideal stepfather but he was better than some. He was rich and at least he didn't drink or hit. Sure, he was unfair a lot of the time: like when he grounded Phoenix for stupid little things like running late for school or not putting his plate in the dishwasher; but Phoenix was prepared to put up with that for his mother's happiness.

With a sigh, Phoenix turned his attention to the latest on-line game he'd joined and did his level best to obliterate both restless unhappiness and digital enemies for the next twenty minutes or so. For some reason, it didn't seem to help this time, so he logged out and switched to updating his blog. Nobody read it but it made him feel better to vent his irritation with Jacob somewhere. Eventually, even the satisfaction of that wore off and he watched some of the weird stuff that came up on YouTube, instead.

Footsteps sounded on the stairs – heavy ones.

Phoenix glanced at the door. There was only one reason for Jacob to come upstairs – to see his stepson, and that was not good news. He cleaned away the debris of food and tossed the Coke can into the bin. He wasn't supposed to eat in his room. Brushing crumbs off his shirt, Phoenix closed his blog and YouTube and jumped to his feet just as the door handle turned.

The door opened and Jacob filled the space with his bulk. Phoenix tried to resist the urge to back away. His stepfather was intimidating – a fact he knew and used to his advantage both at work and at home. It was hard not to feel young and defenceless when faced with Jacob's six foot, muscular form.

Familiar resentment burned low in Phoenx's guts. He swallowed hard, pushing the feelings down. Maybe in a few years time he'd be big enough and tough enough to take Jacob on but until then…

"Did you take the last Coke?" Jacob's grey eyes were

narrowed in annoyance.

Dumbly, Phoenix nodded, trying to slow his now-racing heart. "Sorry."

Jacob grunted, his gaze darting around the room. He spotted the pizza container Phoenix had forgotten to hide. His mouth thinned. With two long strides he walked over and brandished it in Phoenix's face like a weapon.

"And my pizza. I was saving it for lunch tomorrow," he growled.

Phoenix tried to hold his head up defiantly but couldn't. He looked away and was ashamed of his own cowardice. "Sorry," he mumbled again. "I didn't know."

Jacob moved closer. Phoenix took an involuntary step away and sat down as the chair caught him in the back of the knees. His stepfather leaned over him, placing huge hands on the chair arms.

"I'm sick of your attitude, Phoenix," he said, his expression stiff with barely-restrained annoyance. "You're lazy and self-centred and you act as though the world owes you a living. Lord knows I've tried to be patient for your mother's sake but enough is enough. If you want to continue to live in my house then you'll live by my rules, understand?" He waited a moment until Phoenix managed a nod then he pushed off and stood up. "If not then you're welcome to go elsewhere." With a glare, Jacob turned on his heel and left, slamming the door.

Phoenix made a rude gesture at the door then slumped back in the chair, gritting his teeth stop himself from yelling an angry comeback as well. It just wasn't fair. It was hard enough to cope with high school, homework; and idiot older kids at school bullying the younger ones without getting it at home as well. If his real dad was alive this wouldn't be happening.

He glanced at a framed photo on his desk. Alex Carter grinned back at him, his arm around a younger Phoenix, both of them smiling madly and holding up a large, silvery trout. That had been such a great camping trip. The three of them had trekked around the Scottish highlands for two weeks, camping and fishing wherever they felt like it. Phoenix grimaced. His mother had complained about the rain. His father had hugged her, smiled at her and promised her a week in the south of France sunshine for their next holiday. Gwen Carter laughed and shook her damp head knowingly before sending her two boys off to catch dinner. Somehow, when they returned, cold and triumphant, she had a fire going and hot chocolate ready.

That night, the clouds cleared and Alex took his son and wife to lie in the heather and watch the stars. Shooting stars arced like fireworks through the brilliant skies. His father pointed out constellations and told stories of ancient cultures and their beliefs in sky-gods. Phoenix had listened, fascinated by his father's gift for weaving stories and fact into vivid images. Eventually, when they were all chilled and tired, he had gone to sleep in their little tent, hearing the laughing, contented murmured conversation of his parents as they sat by the fire.

There was a noise downstairs: the kitchen door closing; his mother's cheerful voice upraised in greeting. Depression descended on Phoenix again like the Scottish clouds. A faint surge of old anger washed through him. He reached up and lay his father's photo face down on the desk. Alex Carter was gone. Things would never be the same again. He was stuck with this life until he was old enough to get the heck out. Slow tears stung his eyes but he clenched his fists and took deep breaths until the pain subsided. He would not cry. Crying was for kids and he hadn't been a kid for three years now.

"Phoenix, I'm home!" The lilting sound of his mother's voice rescued him. His mother's light footsteps sounded outside his room. Phoenix hastily pulled out a math book and opened it. In answer to her cautious knock, he told her to come in and swivelled around to face the door, forcing a smile.

Gwen Carter-Smithson peeked around the door, her pretty face worried. "Jacob said you two had another run-in." She came in hesitantly and sat on his bed, laying two wrapped parcels down to one side. "Are you ok?"

Phoenix gave her a one-shoulder shrug and turned his face away, afraid she'd see the resentment there. "I ate his pizza by accident. He was angry at me. I'll live."

"Oh, honey." She put a soft hand on his knee. "He really does try, you know, and you could be a little easier on him if you wanted. I know he's not your Dad but he is doing his best."

Hurt she was siding with Jacob, he swung his chair so her hand slid off his knee. He pulled up his messages again and pretended to read one. Behind him, his mother sighed faintly.

"I've got a surprise for you," she offered.

Closing his eyes for a second, Phoenix turned back around and tried to look pleased as he took a thick rectangular package from her hands. "What's this for?"

Gwen smiled and shook her smooth blonde head, "Nothing. I just saw this in town and thought you might like it."

He shook it a little and looked up at her knowingly.

His mother faked a pout. "You've guessed, haven't you? I knew I should have wrapped it differently. You always guess. You're too smart for me." She smiled. "Go on, open it anyway"

Phoenix ripped open the silver paper to reveal a computer game. He managed to work up a little enthusiasm when he realised it was the Pre-release of the newest fantasy game: 80AD. Some kids at school had been raving about it just today. It wasn't due for full release for another two days. He'd only be able to footle about on Level One until the Internet Servers allowed access to the full version midnight on Sunday night, so this could be fun.

Flipping it over, he read the description. The usual Quest-type game set in ancient times with wizards, dragons, gods, heroes and five levels of difficulty. It did come with a set of Virtual reality glasses and a Body Connect receiver, which was extremely cool. He could stand in front of the screen, see the image in surround vision and the receiver would interpret his body movements realistically - so he could kick and punch the badguys in the game to his heart's content without having to use a joystick or mouse. The graphics looked pretty good and there were probably already cheat-sites on the web he could look up. Should be interesting for a few hours, anyway.

"Thanks, mum," he said as brightly as he could manage. "It looks great. I'll load it in a minute. What's this?" He fingered the second package, frowning. It was about the size of his palm but hard and square like a small box.

"Well, if you can't guess I'm sure not going to tell you!" Gwen grinned, her pink cheeks dimpling. "Open it and see. It's something your father gave me before you were born. I've been holding onto it for you. I figured this was a good time to give it to you. You've grown up so fast these last couple of years." She looked at him with a hint of regret.

Tearing off the paper, Phoenix wasn't really paying attention to the gift until it fell into the palm of his hand. It was a small box of some dark wood, inlaid with ornate decorations of pearl and some whitish-green stone. The decorations looked kind of like long, thin dragons and birds twisting around the shiny black lid. It was clipped shut with a tarnished silver hook. It looked old but it was probably just some cheap "made in China" replica antique. Still…

He raised an eyebrow and glanced up at his mother. She nodded for him to open it. Flicking the clasp open with his thumb, he lifted the lid and drew a deep breath of admiration. Lying on a worn bed of worn red cloth was a necklace: a thin silver chain with a teardrop shaped pendant hanging off it. Actually, it was a tadpole-shape. The thick, rounded end hung from the chain and a kind of curved tail pointed sort of down and sideways. It was only about the size of a small coin. The metal had a strange sort of pearly sheen to it and there was a dot of some other, golden metal in the middle of the thicker end. When he turned it in the light, purples and blues and pinks slipped across the surface like oil.

It was fascinating; beautiful, somehow…odd...and warm to the touch.

Anger forgotten, Phoenix glanced at his mother again. She stared at the pendant with a puzzled expression. Then she shook herself and plucked it from his hand. Briskly, she clasped the chain around his neck and tucked the pendant inside his shirt. Patting his chest, she kissed the top of his head. He could see in the mirror on his wardrobe she had tears in her eyes.

"Your father gave this to me on our second date," she sighed. "I only ever took it off once, to get it cleaned, about two hours before he died."

"I remember you wearing it. Where did you get it?" Phoenix pulled it out to look at it again.

"We were wandering through an antique store in London and found them tucked away in that little box in the corner of an old dresser. I've always liked boxes."

"Them?" Phoenix looked up at her. "Hang, on. Dad wore one, too, didn't he? I remember now."

His mother nodded. Her mouth pulled down at the corners. "They were a pair." She traced her finger down the inside curved edge of the amulet. "They fit together perfectly. Mine was silvery and his was a gold colour but each has a dot of the other colour inside." She touched the tiny dot of gold. "It's the Chinese Yin Yang symbol, you know. For balance and harmony. It was supposed to bring us happiness in our marriage, although your dad always said '*happiness is a journey, not a destination*'. You know how he always quoted those old Chinese sayings."

Phoenix nodded, smiling at the memory of some of his father's more obscure proverbs. He still had no idea what half of them meant. "Yeah. I remember his favourite: '*you often find your destiny in the very place you seek to hide from it.*'"

Gwen nodded then sighed. "They did bring us happiness – right up until the time I took it off and he died."

"Mum!" Phoenix protested. "You don't really think taking a necklace off had anything to do with the accident?"

"No, of course not," she said. "It was just an unlucky co-incidence." Gwen shook herself and stood up. "Unfortunately, on the day your dad died, his half disappeared. The paramedics thought the chain must have broken in the car accident and either someone picked it up or it got swept up by the street cleaners." She frowned. "I've always wondered if it was those two oddly-dressed people that were seen with your dad just before he died...." She shook her head and sighed again.

Phoenix shifted on his seat, not knowing what to say.

"Anyway..." With a bright smile, she leaned down to kiss him again. "Happy anythingday."

"Thanks, Mum." He held up the amulet. "This is the best gift ever. I promise I'll take care of it."

She smiled sadly and nodded. "I know you will. You're a good ki...young man." Kissing him again, she moved toward the door. "I'll go so you can play your game. Do come down in time for dinner, though. Chef's making your favourite."

"OK." Phoenix watched the door close then stared at the half-amulet around his neck. It was warm. Maybe that was just because it was against his skin. Or maybe it felt that way because his father was somehow still connected to it, watching over him.

The sound of his stepfather's voice downstairs made Phoenix shake his head irritably. How stupid. There was nobody watching over him. His father was dead; his mother married to an idiot; his life reduced to escaping into computer games whenever he could. Destiny. Ha. Some destiny. With a twist to his mouth, Phoenix found the game's beta site and started to read the instructions.

****

CHAPTER TWO

JADE

"Amber! Crystal! Jewel! Have you seen Jade?"

The shrill voice from the kitchen made Jade shrink further into the darkness. She bit her lip, staring hopefully at the bottom of the stairs close overhead. She hadn't tried this hiding place before. Maybe they wouldn't find her.

"Jaaaaade! Jaaaaaade! Mum wants you!" At the sound of three girlish voices and six feet thumping up the stairs, Jade gritted her teeth. If only she could find somewhere to be alone!

"Jade Pearl Lockyer get your backside out here this minute!"

She sighed and pushed open the tiny storage cupboard door with her foot. There was no point in hiding when her mother took that tone. She really should be helping out for the party anyway. Besides, it was a waste of a good hiding place. No-one else knew about this secret, small cupboard under the stairs and it even had a light. She'd managed to stash a few books and some food in there earlier. Maybe she could sneak back and get away from her noisy, irritating family for a while, later.

"I'm here, Mum!" she yelled, closing the almost-invisible door behind her and brushing dust off her clothes. Stomping into the kitchen, she blinked at the chaos and barely protested when her mother dumped a huge bag of potatoes into her hands.

"Good. About time. Peel these and wash them. There's only two hours until the party and I have to make potato salad to take." Her mother turned back and directed one of the other girls to cut up celery.

Jade wrestled a stool away from Amber. She sat down at the big kitchen bench, ignoring her older sister's childish protests. Glowering, Jade snatched up a potato peeler and began peeling. Annoyance faded a little when she realised she hadn't washed her hands. Ha! Maybe everyone at Coral's party would get botulism. Lost in a pleasant daydream where she somehow managed to save everyone at the engagement party from the horrors of food poisoning, Jade worked steadily through half the bag.

"OOOOooooowww!" A screeching howl of pain snatched her back to reality. Ruby clutched at her hand, yowling like a banshee while her mother and the other girls twittered around in helpless indecision. An angry red burn marred Ruby's sister's hand where she'd tipped hot water on herself.

Jade dropped a half-peeled potato, snatched up a knife and ran out the back door. Slicing off the thick leaf of a plant by the door, she raced back. She slipped the knife along the length of the leaf, exposing a gooey jelly inside. She wormed her way through the throng of chattering girls and grabbed the burned hand. Before Ruby could protest, Jade slathered the yellowish jelly over the burn. Ruby sighed in relief. With smile of pride, Jade turned to her watching family.

Her mother blinked in astonishment. "What is that disgusting stuff?" she demanded. Jade's heart sank and she looked around to find all six of her older sisters and her mother staring at her like a bunch of clones – all with the same expression of wary distaste on their pretty faces.

"It's aloe vera. Perfect for burns. I planted some about two months ago, right by the back door just in case of an emergency...like...this." She tried hard not to let worry creep into her voice. She had done the right thing. Why couldn't her mother see that? Jade stared at her toes as her mother rolled her eyes in disgust. No matter how hard she tried, nothing she did was good enough.

All her older sisters were prettier than she: all blonde, curvy and blue-eyed; all with boyfriends, friends and full social calendars. The whole family looked on their youngest sibling as some sort of freak. Jade had short, wavy dark hair and green eyes. At almost fourteen she was thin and wiry. All her sisters had already been young women at the same age. Sometimes she thought she must be adopted; but who in their right mind would adopt a seventh girl?

"Everything alright in here Allison, ladies?" a mild voice inquired from the kitchen door.

Jade's father stood there and she knew she wasn't adopted. All her sisters were younger versions of her mother. She was the spitting image of her father. She looked to him for support, while her mother replied in a cross tone.

"It's only Jade showing off again, Hector. Honestly. You shouldn't encourage her." Allison Lockyer huffed and turned back to settle Ruby on a chair in the corner. "Get back to work, girls. Coral, you get up to your room and get changed. Hurry!" Glancing at her watch, she cast a despairing look around the chaotic kitchen. Her eye fell on the half-peeled potatoes and she groaned. "Jade, that stuff had better not stain your shirt. Quit fussing with your stupid herbs and get back to the potatoes. We all have to be in the car in an hour and a half."

Jade caught her father's ironic gaze and tried to hide the hurt she felt at her mother's dismissal. He smiled slightly and nodded at the aloe leaf still in her hand. With that tiny smile he acknowledged her quick thinking before retreating back to his study. She relaxed. Dad understood. She resumed her work, almost content.

She could hardly wait to get this party over with so she could help him in the glasshouse with the latest exotic specimen he'd brought back from South America. Spending time helping Dad prepare and study plants for his botany students at Cambridge was way more rewarding than peeling potatoes. Dad never criticised her. If only he didn't have to go away so much. Home was no fun at all when he was gone. Maybe she could just stow away on his next trip and be his assistant.

That nice little daydream ended when her mother caught sight of the still-unpeeled potatoes.

"Jade! Concentrate on what you're doing. Finish those potatoes."

She sighed, hunching her shoulders. She'd never be able to live up to her mother's expectations. Why was it so awful to read or mess about with plants instead of buy dresses and try on makeup? Why did she even bother to try?

Jade finished peeling the potatoes and glanced around. Everyone was frantically busy and no-one was watching. She stole out of the kitchen and made for the cupboard again. Maybe if she was very, very quiet, no one would notice and they would all bustle off to the party without her. Just the thought of having the whole, entire house to herself made Jade hug herself in delight. No sisters to tease her and steal her books; no mother to shake her head in despair.

It was a small house; old and full of secrets. They'd only lived here a year and so far she'd discovered an attic full of discarded bits of other people's lives, a secret drawer in the fireplace mantle (regrettably empty) and now this secret cupboard under the stairs. Her retreats to the attic hadn't lasted long but they'd been full of imaginary adventure. Who had slept in the tiny, broken cot? Whose favourite toy had been the wooden doll with painted eyes? A wooden sword had given her hours of enjoyment battling ancient dragons and knights.

Then her sisters had discovered her and the magic had been lost in their exclamations of disgust. It was so dusty and gross up there. Ewwww! They'd said. Their mother came up and stripped the place bare. What was saleable was auctioned on Ebay. What wasn't went to the dump. The doll, the cot. Gone. Jade managed to hide the sword in the back of her closet but now there was nowhere to play with it. The attic was converted into a retreat for the older girls and Jade banned until she turned sixteen.

So, the cupboard under the stairs was all that remained secret. Jade smiled a little as she crept into it. She felt like Harry Potter but she was hiding out by choice. Oh, how she longed to be like Harry and disappear off to a magical school of wizardry. Did being the seventh daughter of a seventh son make her magic? Or maybe to someplace where she could train to be a knight. Maybe not. That armour looked pretty heavy.

She picked up the book she'd been reading.

*

It was the sudden silence that roused her from a world of fantasy. Listening, she cocked her head. The house was silent. Worried, she pushed open the cupboard door and darted out.

"Mum!? Dad?" Her voice echoed. There was no reply. No footsteps. No noise at all. They really had left without her.

Her first reaction was one of delight. No stupid, boring engagement party. No being "good" for hours on end in company. No having to listen to dumb speeches about Coral and her fiancé. No having to fetch and carry and play waitress; and, especially, no princessy, perfect sisters swanning about making her feel ugly and clumsy. She had the whole house to herself!

"Yahooo!" Executing a neat dance step, Jade shimmied down the hall, singing the theme song to a weekend cartoon, "I'm strange, and I like it; that's just the way I am..." In quick succession, she peeked into each room of the bottom floor, just to make certain she was alone. She was. Everyone was gone. The big old house was totally empty. Completely, totally empty, except for her...

Very empty.

Maybe too empty...

Jade stood still in the middle of the entrance hallway, listening. The wind picked up outside. That must be what caused that strange whooooooing sound. Yes, it was just the wind going past the chimney stack. That rattling...well, that had to be a window one of the girls had left open upstairs. Honestly, she fumed, how thoughtless they were.

She turned and placed a foot on the bottom stair, ready to go up and latch the window. Darkness cloaked the top landing. All the lights were turned off. It's just darkness, she admonished herself firmly. She took another step upward, trying to ignore the sudden flutter of her heart.

Somewhere up there, a floorboard creaked; then another. Swallowing, Jade backed down again, into a corner of the hall, where she huddled with arms around her thin body. These were not the noises she was used to hearing in this house. She was so used to the sounds of her six sisters chattering and fighting that it was unnatural not to hear them. It didn't make her feel better to tell herself that all old houses made creaking noises. The wind outside was now fairly howling and rain pelted against the timber walls. The window rattled again.

A shrill jangling, right beside her, made her leap a foot into the air and let out a shriek. The telephone. Taking a deep breath, she reached for the ancient handset, and then paused. Should she answer it or not? Images of horror movies jumped into her head. People left home alone and stalked by axe-murderers. What if it was her parents calling because they realised they'd left her?

What if it wasn't?

Her hand hovered over the handset for five full rings before she snatched it up. "H.Hello?"

"Are you alright, honey?" Her dad's worried tones sounded hollow and far away. A rushing noise in the background almost drowned him out.

"Dad!" Jade let out the breath she'd been holding and sat down on the telephone stool in relief. The house seemed almost ordinary again. "I'm fine. You guys left without me!"

"Sorry honey. Your mum was in such a hurry we didn't count heads."

"Are you coming back for me?" Jade heard giggling. Oh! Her sisters had known she was missing and had deliberately not told their parents. Biting her lip, she struggled not to cry. They were so mean.

"We really can't. We're already going to be late for Coral's engagement party as it is." He sounded regretful. Jade heard her mother's voice clearly, complaining about her youngest daughter's complete lack of consideration for others. Her father hushed her mother loudly and Jade choked back tears of hurt. She felt guilty about causing so much trouble but it really hadn't been on purpose. Surely her father knew that?

"Dad?" She sniffed. "I didn't do it on purpose."

"It's ok, honey," he reassured her. "I've called Mrs Nevin and she's going to come over to babysit until we get home. She won't be there for about an hour, though. Can you manage?"

She nodded, forgetting he couldn't see her. "Sure, Dad," she said morosely. "I'll be fine. I don't really need a sitter." Even as she said it, Jade realised that she was quite glad Mrs Nevin was coming over. She'd never let her sisters know that.

"I know but I'd feel better if you had someone with you," he replied. "We'll be pretty late getting home." She could hear the pride and worry making his voice smile.

She gave in. "OK but…"

"Yes?"

"Can I play that new computer game you got yesterday?" Dad never ever let anyone play on his computer. It was the only decent, new computer they owned and he didn't want to risk it getting broken. "Please?"

He chuckled. "Alright, but you know the deal?"

"I know." She giggled, happier now. "Don't let the others know. As if they'd want to play computer games anyway, Dad."

"Don't be cheeky or I'll change my mind." He spoke sternly but she heard the smile in his voice again. "Be good. Call us if you get scared before Mrs Nevin gets there."

"I'll be fine, Dad." Jade said more confidently than she felt. "I'm almost fourteen, remember?"

"How could I forget? Bye honey."

"Bye Dad. Thanks." She hung up the phone and bounced up, excited all over again. She clapped her hands and raced toward her father's study without looking up the dark stairs. Her sisters could keep their stupid party. She was going to create the most beautiful, kick-ass avatar in history, play 80AD and defeat the evil villain Feng Zhudai.

Jade was almost there when she spotted the door to the under-stairs cupboard. Golden light streamed out the half-open door for the girls to see when they came home. That wouldn't do at all. Hurrying back, she reached around and felt for the light switch.

Instead of the switch, her fingers encountered something soft tucked into a corner of the wooden beams that lined the tiny room. Ducking her head in, she tried to see, but her head blocked the light. She had to wiggle the item out of its hiding place by feel alone. There was only a tiny piece sticking out, so it took a bit of work to get it all free.

Finally, she held in her hand a small, green velvet bag. The sort a jeweller might put a trinket into at the craft markets. It couldn't be very old, because the bag was in perfect condition. The pull-tie strings at the neck were even finished with little plastic bits like shoestrings.

Still…

Anticipation quivered in her belly as she tugged at the neck of the bag. Who had hidden it? What was in it? Why was it so carefully secreted away? Was it dangerous? Magical maybe?

Taking a deep breath, she got a firm grip on her imagination. Her father always laughed at her wild stories. The bag slid open and she tipped it onto the palm of her hand. Out slithered a fine gold necklace with a pendant on it.

Touching it with a gentle finger, she drew a slow, reverent breath. The shape looked familiar somehow. It was a kind of bent gold teardrop shape with a pearly silver dot on one end. The delicate chain threaded through a tiny loop in the skinny end of the drop. It was beautiful and sort of warm to touch.

Inspecting the chain, she discovered the clasp was broken and it was marked with smudges of a dark rusty coloured stuff that flaked off on her fingers. Jade touched the chain hanging around her own neck. A gift from her father on her 10th birthday. It wasn't nearly as pretty as the one in her hand but at least it was whole and clean. Quickly, before she changed her mind, she slipped the pendant off its chain and onto her own.

She glanced at it once more before tucking it safely inside her t-shirt. There was now a small, warm spot on her chest where the pendant lay. Guiltily, she glanced around. She half-expected the real owner to show up and demand her property any moment. That was silly. The previous owners were a very old couple who had lived in the house for twenty years or more. They didn't have any children or even any grandchildren whose nimble fingers might have hidden the necklace away.

It certainly was a puzzle. Who could have put it there? One of her sisters? She hoped not. She didn't want to have to share her hiding place or this secret treasure.

Jade chewed her bottom lip then tucked the broken chain and bag into her pocket. She really didn't want to give the pendant back, but she didn't like feeling guilty about keeping it. She switched off the light and slid the door shut. Tomorrow she'd show it to her father and he could tell her what to do. Yes. That was the right thing. Feeling better, Jade went to her father's study – via the refrigerator for a snack.

****

CHAPTER THREE

LET THE GAME BEGIN

Right. Character selection. Phoenix put the VR headset aside for a moment and scrolled the mouse pointer down the screen, scanning the list of character types with idle interest. If he was going to play, he wanted to be something strong; something invincible. There: the Warrior. Yes.

Choosing carefully, he equipped his hero with a long sword, iron-studded leather armour, a shield and a dagger. What else would an adventurer need to survive in the old days? This game seemed a lot more complex than he'd thought. It wasn't just your simple Quest-with-lots-of-fighting. In those, all you had to do was kill things. This was an on-line, role-playing, game where you had hundreds of choices and decisions to make about everything and each choice affected how the game went. Of course, you still got to kill things, otherwise what was the point, really?

He had to plan for long trips and bad weather, for hunger and thirst, for hunting and sleeping outdoors. It was pretty cool, actually, but it did his head in trying to think of what someone living off the land two thousand years ago might need. He added a water skin, a coil of thin rope, boots, shirts and breeches, a thick travelling cloak, flint and tinder box and a small sling for hunting. There didn't seem to be an option for underwear. Maybe Warriors didn't wear underwear. He grinned at the thought, his earlier depression slipping away as he got involved in the game setup.

Hmmmm. He needed a name. He couldn't keep thinking of him as "hero" or "warrior". With a wry grin, Phoenix typed his own name in the field. "The Phoenix." It sounded more like a modern superhero so he deleted the "The" and left just his own name. Now at least he could pretend his life was different.

OK. Other characteristics. There were random dice-roll buttons to choose for things like intelligence, charisma, health, strength, dexterity and looks. The result could be anything from two to twenty. A Two meant you were really stupid while a Twenty meant you were a genius. You could roll the dice only three times for each attribute. If you didn't like the third attempt, it was just too bad.

Phoenix pushed the "roll" button for Intelligence. Whew, a fifteen. Quickly he hit "Save". Fifteen out of twenty was pretty good – especially for a warrior. Next was Charisma. He switched out of the game for a moment and looked the word "Charisma" up in the online dictionary. It said: *those special qualities that give someone the ability to influence or impress others. From the ancient Greek word "Kharis" meaning "grace"*.

So it was kind of like charm or interestingness, if there was such a word. Well, surely it wouldn't be so bad if that were a bit low. It wasn't as though a Warrior spent much time chatting and impressing people he was trying to kill. He stuck with the fourteen that came up second roll. His Health and Looks came out as average, which was fine.

After that, he had to resort to the dictionary again to find out what Dexterity was. It meant how quick and skilful his character was on his feet or with his hands. He was a bit disappointed to only get a fourteen for that after three tries. It meant his Warrior would be just average and that wasn't great for a swordsman. Maybe he could get better. The rules said as you went up levels you could improve some of your attributes. For Strength he rolled twenty the first time, saving it with a fierce grin of triumph and an unexpected surge of relief. He would kick butt!

Finally, he Saved the character and quit the game temporarily. It was time to hunt up some Cheat-sites on the

Net. OK, so it was a bit wrong to cheat but it was only a computer game. What harm was there?

Phoenix realised he was arguing with himself and shook his head. It was like hearing his father's voice in his head, urging him to always "do the right thing, not the easy thing." Had his father even known that sometimes doing the right thing got you nowhere? Probably not, he thought with easy scorn. He'd never had to deal with someone like Jacob. Jacob didn't do the right thing, so why should Phoenix? Stubbornly, Phoenix began searching for the cheat-sites.

Unfortunately, being still in Pre-release, there wasn't much out there yet but he tagged a few sites that had some useful hints before re-entering the beta version. After a deep breath, he pushed his chair out of the way, stood and put on the VR headset. It was a full-face unit, so he saw the 80AD world in all directions, like he was really in it. He turned around and the view changed, showing what lay behind his avatar. Cool. The image of grass, a dirt road, and forest was so vivid he had to raise the mask for a moment just to be sure he was still in his room. Amazing. The graphics were brilliant - still a little on the too-smooth side as with all digital stuff but better than most others on the market. The earphones built into the headset even gave out sounds - birds twittering, small animals rustling in the underbrush, the wind in the trees.

Phoenix raised his right hand so that his avatar's hand appeared in front of his face. It held a sword. He grinned, swishing it around experimentally. This was almost as good as actually being there. With this, he could imagine he was in 80AD. In fact, it took no imagination at all. Totally freaking awesome. For a long moment, he stared around and let himself pretend he really was there, in another world, living another life, being the all-conquering hero. It was a thrilling idea. He wished it were true; wished he could somehow transport himself inside the game and be

Phoenix the kick-ass warrior hero for a while.

With a sigh, he shook his head, hit the BEGIN button and waited to see what would happen.

He lost himself in the game. He missed dinner. Against the standing rule about eating in his room, his mother brought up a cold plate of food and a piece of cake. He barely heard her quiet "dinner, honey" and didn't hear her leave his room. He was kicking butt big time. He couldn't wait for the full release so he could work through all five levels. It promised to be even better.

He spent a while wandering about the woods beating up bandits in a very satisfying way before running into a two-man Roman patrol. A short, nasty fight left one soldier dead and Phoenix's avatar with a deep wound on his left arm. The other soldier ran away. Phoenix figured it was more important to get his arm fixed, than give chase, so he tore a strip from his shirt to tie around the wound then headed toward a small village. He'd worked up a sweat anyway, so he sat down so he could eat, and switched the game to keyboard mode.

Character Notes on the heads-up display of the VR set told him his hero was thirsty and hungry as well. It took a while but he finally worked out that a round, thatch-roofed mud-house with a bit of dried plant hanging off a signpost had to be the local tavern.

What a sight it was inside. He'd been expecting a pub like the one in town – with tiled floors, a long polished bar and a big screen television, lots of clean glasses and bottles lined up in fridges.

Of course, this was England of two thousand years before – although it was called 'Albion' back then, not 'England'. The game rules said Level One was set in pre-Christian, Iron Age Britain of 80AD. That put it shortly after the Roman invasion. Agricola, the Roman Governor of Britain, was busy squashing the local Celtic tribes in short, brutal battles. It was a dark, unsettled period in

British history to which the game programmers had added fantasy elements – elves, dwarves, trolls, dragons and the like.

No bars or fridges.

No electricity or cars.

No filtered water or softdrinks.

Instead, the tavern was dark and smoky with a few rough benches and tables set around a central fire. Stray bits of straw drifted down from the thatched roof, adding to the general filth of the packed earth floor. Cups and plates of clumsy clay rested on heavy tables of unfinished wood. Some sort of thin ale was poured from big barrels by a suspicious-eyed tavern-keeper. Phoenix got his Warrior to drink it, half-wishing he could really taste it. It was probably disgusting, though.

Through the headset, he could even hear the coarse laughter of the customers and the barks of dogs that roamed freely over the floor. It was impressive. The graphics really were superb. He decided to stay and eat, too. The tavern-keeper served him a watery soup. Phoenix didn't want to know what the floaty bits were. He glanced at his own real dinner and nibbled gratefully at a slice of roast beef.

Finally, he noticed blood seeping through the bandage on his digital arm and decided he'd better find a doctor. As he headed for the door, the tavern-keeper yelled at him, demanding payment for the ale and food. It was only then that Phoenix realised what he'd forgotten: money. His warrior had none. He stared blankly at the screen, wondering what to do next. The tavern-keeper took grudging pity on him and said that if he'd chop wood he could pay off the debt.

Phoenix thought seriously about telling him to go jump in a lake. Couldn't he see the Warrior was wounded? What right did he have to make him work like some sort of slave just to pay for a drink and some pigslop soup? Just as he opened his mouth to give a nasty answer, another person entered the tavern. All the talking stopped and every CGI man in the room turned to look at the stranger.

It was a girl; and not just an ordinary tavern wench, either - whatever they looked like. This girl was the most beautiful thing Phoenix had ever seen. Even with the slightly unreal look of computer graphics, she was still extraordinary. He couldn't help but stare.

She wore a rough-woven brown, hooded cloak that didn't completely hide her slanted green eyes and long fair hair. As he looked closely, he realised she must be another Player. All of the Players had a small P embroidered somewhere on their clothes, to help others identify them. Hers showed on the left shoulder of her dark green tunic. His was embossed on the leather of his character's armour.

He grinned when the tavernkeeper abandoned him and bustled up to the girl, demanding to know what she wanted. Apparently, women weren't allowed in the taverns. She asked for food, jingling a full belt-pouch to show she could pay for it. Silence fell again as the villagers eyed her now with a different kind of greed. Even the kitchen boy, who had served Phoenix his food, stopped in mid-stride to stare hungrily at her. She seemed startled and glanced around. Phoenix felt, for a second, that she'd looked right at him, straight out of the computer screen and actually at him. He shivered. The amulet on his chest was warm. It seemed to be getting warmer, too.

Distracted, he fingered it.

After a moment's hesitation, the tavernkeeper refused to serve her and turned away. Looking lost, the girl headed back toward the front door, only to be stopped by three large peasant-types. They were led by a smaller man; thin, with a pointed, weasel-face and shrewd dark eyes.

"There's a toll for the likes of you, wench," he sneered.

She backed away, holding her hands up in a peaceful gesture. In one, she carried a quarterstaff.

"I just came in to get food and shelter from the storm,"

she said. "I don't want any trouble."

Phoenix almost laughed. Why was she Playing this sort of game if she didn't want trouble? This would be interesting. He leaned against a post, watching.

The peasants closed in on her. Other patrons sensed what was coming and hastily got out of the way, tossing down their drinks and sliding out of the room. The innkeeper groaned and packed away breakables as fast as he could.

Phoenix grinned widely. A bar fight. Now this was more like it.

As her four attackers spread out to encircle her, the girl turned, trying to keep them all in sight. She changed her grip on the quarterstaff, holding it crossways in front of her body. For a few tense moments, action was suspended, as everyone froze, watching her.

One of the men launched himself toward her. She reacted in a blur of movement. Thump! The end of her staff punched out, catching him directly in the solar plexus. He flew backward to slide bonelessly down a wall, gasping for breath that would not come.

It happened so fast that the other three were still moving toward her. Now she stepped into the gap she'd created and could see all three of them at once. Phoenix nodded approvingly. She might just make it after all.

He straightened up, frowning. The smallest man wasn't playing fair. He slid around and came at her from behind by crawling under one of the bench-tables. He had a dagger in his hand and clearly intended to stab her in the back.

Thwack! Another foe dropped at her feet, felled by a perfect blow to the head. Phoenix almost applauded out loud. Instead, he called out a warning to her.

"Behind you!"

She spun, twirling the staff gracefully in an arc over her head. It came down across the weasel-faced man's outstretched hand. Bones broke with an audible crunch.

The would-be murderer whimpered, clutching at his arm as he backed away. Casting Phoenix a venomous glare, he jerked his head at his remaining crony and the two edged away. Keeping the girl in sight, they retreated out the front door.

It slammed shut behind them, leaving the bar empty except for her, Phoenix and the kitchen boy, who had observed everything with a gap-toothed smile of appreciation.

Clapping, Phoenix hitched himself off the pole and sauntered over. She looked at him warily.

"Nicely done," he said.

She grimaced at the two prone bodies. The tavern-keeper reappeared and began the task of tidying up, muttering to himself and sending them irritated looks.

Phoenix stuck out a hand. "I'm Phoenix." He pointed to the P embossed on his armour so she'd know he was a Player, too.

She relaxed and smiled slightly, shaking his hand. "Jade. Thanks for the warning, by the way."

"You're welcome. Oh, leave it be, would you?" This last comment he addressed to the innkeeper, who had returned and now complained loudly about damage, non-payment of bills and women in the bar. "She's with me, ok?"

The tavernkeeper sent him a scathing look and jerked his head. "Well, if she can pay for yer bill 'o fare and the damage, she can eat, too – out back, though," he said roughly.

"There's a storm coming," she protested. "I need..." she glanced at Phoenix and changed her sentence. "We need shelter."

"Tha's welcome to the barn out back for an extra copper. Jus' don't fret th' cow." The tavernkeeper took her coins and handed her a bowl of soup.

Phoenix followed her out the back door. As they

crossed a bare yard to the small barn, he glanced up at the sky. She was right about the storm. The barn was no more than another mud and thatch hut but at least it was shelter. He hadn't even thought about where his hero would sleep for the night. He hadn't thought about a lot of things, apparently.

They were silent awhile as Jade sat on a hay bale and finished eating. Phoenix tried to ignore the rather scrawny cow tethered in one corner. Somewhere nearby, a chicken squawked irritably, making him jump.

Jade glanced up. "Was that thunder?"

"Err…I thought it sounded more like a chicken." Then there was an unmistakable rumble. Phoenix looked out his real bedroom window and saw lightning. "Hang on. You're right. I've got a real storm here. I should probably shut the game down until it passes."

"I should too, I suppose. It's turning into a nasty one here," she agreed. "Thanks for helping out in there." She nodded at the tavern. "I guess I've got a lot to learn about the customs of Ancient England...er...Albion, I mean."

"No big. You helped me, too." He shrugged. "I forgot to add money to my list of equipment."

Jade laughed. "What about a horse then? Surely you've got one. My character wasn't allowed but yours would be. My virtual feet are killing me." She lifted one boot-shod foot and rubbed it.

Phoenix glared, stung by her laughter. He hadn't thought of getting a horse but that didn't give her the right to laugh at him – especially when he'd just saved one of her lives. The last thing he needed right now was one more person criticising him. He'd been having fun until she came along. He played computer games to escape from real life, not to have to worry about impressing anyone.

He turned away, staring out at the darkening digital sky. A few drops of rain spattered into the dusty yard outside the door. He really wasn't in the right frame of mind for talking. Beating up bandits had exactly suited his mood. He sighed. Maybe he was overreacting. She seemed nice enough, really. It wasn't her fault he was still angry with Jacob.

Mildly irritated that his fun had been spoiled, Phoenix reached up to take the headset off. As he did, something caught his eye in the real world. Looking out the window, he saw a strange sort of shimmery glow shooting down from the heavy storm clouds outside. It looked like slow motion purple lightning. He watched, fascinated as it crackled down toward the tree outside his window and lit the thin branches in an eerie glow. Freaky.

He shook himself and slid the mouse toward the Log Out button on the screen. Best to switch it off with an electrical storm around.

The lightning moved again. It twisted around the branches, slipped through the leaves and wove its way toward the house. Now he got worried. Normal lightning did NOT behave like that. It should have earthed itself on the tree and gone. It wasn't. Instead, it moved up one of the branches that touched the house. Before he could call for help, the light wriggled under his half-open window. He sat perfectly still, totally unable to move or yell. Fearful astonishment held his muscles like a clamp.

The lightning slipped inside and the whole room shimmered in its weird, purple-blue light. It wasn't like a normal lamp where the light comes from one place and casts shadows. Everything glowed. There were no shadows at all. It wasn't super bright, either. Just really, really weird and it felt like it was…looking for something?

The glow condensed back into a thin streak of light. Phoenix cried out as it zipped straight toward him. He backed away, but he still sat in his chair with his VR headset on. Feet tangled in the chair legs and he fell backward. The light pierced his chest. He yelled. A white-hot needle jabbed him in the ribs.

The chair slipped out from beneath him. Phoenix's head hit the floor and everything went dark.

*****

Far away, in the unchanging black, Long Baiyu smiled. A whisper of strength seeped back into his cold, cramped limbs. He raised his heavy head and stared into the blackness.

"Come," he murmured. Resting his head on a forearm, he fell into a natural sleep for the first time in many nights. Now he had a chance.

In luxurious rooms above, his gaoler roared in anger as he, too, sensed a change in the Balance.

****

CHAPTER FOUR

80AD LEVEL ONE

"Phoenix? Phoenix, wake up!" A worried voice dragged him out of sleep. As Phoenix reluctantly opened his eyes, a cool hand touched his forehead. Had he overslept?

"Mum?" He stared vaguely about. His room looked odd. The plain white ceiling had turned into wooden beams with straw over the top. The bed under his body felt like straw, too. What the…?

He sat straight up - and wished he hadn't. His head ached, his arm hurt and his stomach turned flip-flops. Swallowing hard, he peered around, trying to work out what was wrong with everything. OK, he wasn't in his room, that was obvious. Even apart from that, the world looked kind of…odd. It was sort of too smooth, too perfect. Yet, at the same time, it looked a little bit grainy – like a photo that's been made too big so you can see the little square pixels of colour.

"Phoenix? Are you alright?"

He turned his head toward the voice and his mouth flopped open. The woman standing over him wasn't his mother. It was that character from the computer game, Jade. She was even more beautiful close up.

"You're beautiful." He blinked several times. He had to be hallucinating.

She blushed, pressing long fingers to red cheeks and glancing down at her well-curved body. She looked about seventeen.

"I know. It's ridiculous. This body feels all wrong."

"Huh…?" He reached out a hand and carefully touched her arm. She looked odd, like the rest of this place, but she felt real: the rough fabric of her tunic and the warmth of her skin. Was she a real person and who'd come to visit him for some reason? Had he been struck by the weird lightning? Was he in some sort of hospital?

Phoenix glanced about again and dismissed that thought. This was no hospital. Not unless cows had become doctors and chickens, nurses. The tiny candle lantern that lit the room was feeble, but he could see clearly enough. Two fowl roosted in one corner of what was obviously a barn. A skinny cow munched calmly on hay nearby.

Not just any barn. Not just any cow. Memory returned and he gasped aloud at the realisation of exactly where he was – but couldn't possibly be.

"It's the barn behind the tavern! But how? That's a computer game. I don't understand!" He grabbed his head as pain shot through it. His left arm throbbed. A bloody scrap of cloth was wound around it.

"So you feel like it's real, too?" Jade's expression was both eager and worried.

Phoenix looked down. He snatched up a handful of straw and rubbed it on his skin. It still looked too perfect but it sure felt just like real straw. He sniffed it then bit it. It smelled and tasted just like straw, too. His stomach lurched again as his senses disagreed with each other and confused his brain.

"I guess. It seems real – sort of. I just don't understand how."

"Or why." She slumped down onto the hay bale beside him. "One minute I was sitting in front of my Dad's computer, playing the game. Next minute lightning shoots in the window and suddenly I'm in the game and you're lying unconscious on the floor. You've been asleep for ages."

"That's just what happened to me, except that I tripped over my chair and hit my head." His head still hurt. Gingerly he felt the lump growing on the back of his skull.

They sat in silence for awhile, feeling overwhelmed; listening to the rain pattering down outside the building. It was warm and dry inside but it did smell strongly of cow and dung.

"Is it my imagination…" Jade frowned at the rough wooden walls. "Or is it all getting more real looking."

"Huh?" Phoenix squinted around.

"When I first got here," she said, "it all looked sort of …computerish. Y'know? Too smooth. Too perfect."

He nodded. Long black hair fell in his eyes. He shoved it back impatiently.

"Now it looks more like the real world, don't you think?" She stared about the room, tilting her head to one side.

He did the same, wondering if that made a difference. He blinked in astonishment. She was right. All the too-smoothness was being replaced by the millions of tiny imperfections that people take for granted in real things. Maybe it was changing, or maybe his mind was filling in the blanks to make it more acceptable.

Phoenix didn't know and didn't much care. The un-reality of his situation sank in: he was actually inside the game. In the *freaking* game!

He stood up, a little unsteady as he adjusted to longer, stronger legs. Ignoring the thudding in his head, he looked around with new eyes. He really was inside 80AD. It wasn't possible but here he was. Unless it was a dream, there couldn't be any other explanation.

It wasn't just an escape from reality any more; it was reality. A new, better reality. Freaking awesome!

"We're in the game," he said aloud, staring in wonder at the darkening room. "Actually in the game. Do you know what this means?" He turned to the Player girl, excitement welling up to take the place of bewildered confusion. She stared up at him and shook her head, eyes wide.

His left hand fell naturally onto the hilt of his sword. He gripped it and drew it halfway out of the sheath. "It means we can live the Quest instead of just pretending to. It means we can kill dragons, beat up the badguys, get treasure and basically wreak havoc without any consequences. We can do anything we want. Sweet! This is so totally cool!"

There was a long silence as Phoenix inspected his sword with satisfaction. He swished it through the air experimentally, enjoying the sound and weight of it. Muscles in his arms bulged. This was going to be so great! How many times had he wished he could do what his game characters could? Now he *was* his character. Now he could really kick butt.

"But I don't want to be in the game."

Jade's small, worried comment intruded on his enthusiasm. Phoenix paused, looking down at her in surprise. What gamer didn't want to live the game? This was the ultimate escape. How could she not want to be here? Suddenly, she seemed a lot younger than her beautiful avatar appeared. And a lot more frightened.

He sat down, grinning encouragingly. "Come on. It'll be fun. We can steal the Jewel of Asgard, like you're supposed to do in Level One. Who knows, maybe we could even get right through to Level Five, kill Feng Zhudai and win. This is like, every gamers dream. It'll be great. It's just a game."

She shook her head. "But I only wanted to play for a little while. I've never played games before, really. I don't even know what you're supposed to do. I'd just screw everything up."

Phoenix frowned at her, a sudden realisation kicking in. "Hang on," he pointed at the P on her clothing. "You can't be here, anyway."

She screwed up her nose and shook her head again. "What are you talking about? I thought we'd already established that. The fact that we're in a computer game is just impossible but it's happened and we're stuck with it."

"No." He waved her words aside impatiently. "I mean *you* can't be here. You're another Player."

"So?"

He slapped his forehead at her obtuseness then forced himself to calm down. She'd said she didn't play games much, so she obviously didn't understand.

"80AD is a Pre-release game. It means we can all have limited access to it on the internet servers but the game isn't ready for full multi-level, multi-player interactive playing yet. Players shouldn't be able to see each other at all." Experimentally, he prodded her arm. "You must just be a digital construct. You can't be a Player."

"Ow!" She poked him back, scowling. "Of course I am. Maybe you're not the real one."

"Don't be ridiculous," he scoffed. She kept glaring, so he held up his hands. "OK. OK. Let's prove it. We can both think of something that was on the news today as proof that we've come from the real world."

They did so, Phoenix recalling a story about the latest football grand final, Jade relating one about a whaling ship sinking off Japan. Convinced of their own realness, if not that of their current world, they both sank back onto the hay bales.

Phoenix's earlier elation seeped back into his scattered thoughts, like water finding its way though cracks in a dam. He was in the game. Weird or not, this was just too good an opportunity to miss. He hefted the sword again, a grin of anticipation stretching his mouth.

"D'you know what this means?" He turned back to Jade, eager for her to be as excited as he was.

"You've already asked me that." She sighed.

He ignored her lack of enthusiasm. "It means we've got at least forty-eight hours to kick butt before the game is opened up to the world and we get swamped with other Players." He stood up again, swishing the sword and striking what he hoped were warrior-like poses. "For-ty-eight-hours-of-fun!" Each word was punctuated by a strike at an invisible foe.

"I just want to go home." Jade hunched her shoulders and turned her head away.

He stared at her, his mouth half open in shock. He dropped back onto the bale beside her, his mind suddenly overwhelmed with images and ideas.

"What?" She grabbed his shoulder, seeming worried when he just sat there with his mouth open. "What is it? Have you thought of a way to get us home?"

Phoenix shook his head. "But when you said 'home', I suddenly realised I remember everything." He touched his aching head in wonder. It felt bigger than he recalled; with longer hair. He fingered the scar on his cheek – the scar he'd put on his avatar's face only hours before. That was the moment he fully realised that the body he occupied now was not his usual, awkward, half-grown teenage one. It was his computer-generated Warrior one.

"What do you mean, everything?" Jade blinked at him.

"I remember everything about being me, Phoenix Carter from Cambridge, England." He pointed to his chest. "And I remember everything about being him, Phoenix the Warrior." He slapped his new body, feeling hard muscles for the first time. "I remember wandering about the woods this afternoon, fighting bandits. I remember growing up in a little village near Bedford and training for years with my uncle to be a swordsman. The game gave my character a life history when I created him." Phoenix shook his head. "Now I have both lives in my head and it's confusing the hell out of me. My brain's full."

"Oh." Jade's reply was thoughtful. "I see what you mean. Now that I think about it, I have the same stuff. My character grew up in the great forest to the west. I...I remember the spells she knows; and what herbs grow around here. Wow. I even remember eating that stew from the tavern." She made a face and pretended to throw up.

Phoenix couldn't help but smile a little as he glanced at her. He spotted Jade's pointed ears and pale blonde hair. Her character was an Elf. They were very magical, according to the game rules. That gave him an idea.

"You said you know some spells? If you want to go home so much, why don't you just try magicking yourself back?"

She shook her head with a sigh. "I'm only a half-elf and a minor Spellweaver. I know lots of small spells for healing and a few minor curses to use against enemies but nothing big like that. I…" She trailed off frowning at him.

He wondered if his expression betrayed his utter lack of understanding of anything magical. It must have, for she pulled out a small bag and carefully selected two small leaves from inside. Crushing them in her palm, she mixed in a little water from her waterskin. Closing her eyes, she laid her hand on his bandaged arm. He started to pull away.

She grabbed him and held him still. "Just comfrey leaves. Watch."

A spiky, tingling warmth started under her palm. A faint, purple-blue shimmer wavered around her fingers like a heat haze. The warmth spread up his arm, into his shoulder. Then it stopped. Jade took her hand away and tugged the bandage off. Phoenix blinked in surprise at the smooth skin beneath. It was smeared with blood but undamaged. He flexed his fingers.

"Way cool," he approved. "Thanks. That will sure come in handy here."

"I told you: I don't want to stay here! I like reading fantasy books but that's all. I'm not hero material. I'm just…me." She drooped again, staring morosely at her boots.

"Hey, don't stress. It'll be ok." Phoenix put on his best

reassuring voice. "I'll take care of you." He slid his sword back into its scabbard carefully, trying not to slice his own thumb off. "It's getting dark. We'll stay here tonight. Tomorrow we'll work something out."

There was silence for a while, except for the spatter of drizzling rain and chewing noises from the cow.

Jade straightened, turning her head toward the open door.

"Did you hear something?" she whispered, gripping Phoenix's newly-healed arm with surprising strength.

He listened hard then shook his head. "Just chickens again. It's your imagination."

"No," she said, "I heard something. Elves have better hearing. There's someone outside – sneaking."

"So, what do we do?" He felt suddenly breathless; heart racing. It was one thing to watch this stuff on a flatscreen…

She frowned at him. "I don't know. You're the warrior, aren't you? You just said you'd take care of me."

Stung he stood up, drawing his sword again with an ominous *shing* of metal on metal. Swallowing hard, he faced the door. "Right. You stay back. I'll protect you." He tried to ignore the kernel of doubt in his mind. Could he actually use this sword effectively? Would he know how?

After a moment, Jade stepped up beside him; face pale, knuckles white as she held her staff ready. "There's more than one. I think you'll need help."

Phoenix glanced at her doubtfully. He couldn't help feeling a little relieved but she looked like she might faint at any minute. He didn't think…

There was no more time to think.

Three peasants slid into the room, their eyes glinting with greed. Wearing rough, homespun clothing that was distinctly worse for wear, they crept in on bare feet and carried an assortment of ill-kept, notch-bladed knives and axes. They looked more poverty-stricken than professional.

A fourth man appeared, his right hand swathed in dirty bandages. Phoenix groaned and took a firm grip on his sword-hilt, eyeing the weasel-faced man in disgust.

"Not you again. I see you have some new friends," he mocked. "Didn't the other guys want to get beaten by a girl again?"

"Give us your coin, girl, and you can go free," weaselly ordered, ignoring him. He wasn't holding a weapon now but he looked the sort to have an extra knife hidden somewhere in his baggy clothes – a knife that he would use left-handed if necessary. Phoenix wondered how he knew that. Jade shifted her weight and he brought his attention back where it belonged. This was no time to get distracted.

From the corner of his eye, Phoenix saw her hand begin to move toward her belt pouch. He nudged her with an elbow and shook his head. Something told him these men were not open to easy solutions. They were desperate. This was not going to end well.

"You've taken these guys once, remember? We can do it again," he murmured.

"That was her, not me," she hissed, her voice strained with fear.

"You *are* her now," he reminded her. "You know what to do. Just let it happen. They'd kill us anyway. The Romans are law around here and they're afraid we'll report them."

She paused, nodded and tightened her hold on the staff.

The thief-leader's eyes narrowed. He jerked his head at his companions. "Right then. If that's the way you want it. Have at 'em, lads."

The four peasants launched their attack. As though planned, they split up and moved to encircle the pair. Jade and Phoenix turned back to back, waiting.

"You ok?" Phoenix asked softly, feeling her tremble.

"What do you think?" she replied acidly. One man ran

at her, swinging his own short staff in an arc toward her ribs. "No! I. Want. To. Go. Home!" Each word was punctuated with a sharp crack as her staff found its mark six times in quick succession.

Relieved that she seemed to still be able to use her weapon and wasn't going to have hysterics, Phoenix gave in to the flood of adrenalin that pumped through his body. He grinned at the two attackers facing him. His new body automatically dropped into a fighter's crouch, shield slung on his left arm, sword ready in his right. Then, for a brief moment, he felt confused and wondered if he ought to use aikido instead. He half-stood, ready to move into an aikido fighting stance. One half of his mind fought with the other. The warrior part proved stronger in this new body. It took over, thrusting the real-world Phoenix's impulses aside. He dropped back into the crouch, grinning.

Let them come.

The small man hung back, watching as his bigger companion swung a blunt Roman sword at Phoenix's head. This peasant obviously had little training. Phoenix waited until the last second. He took a half-step forward and to the right, turning just enough to deflect the descending blade with his shield. He brought his own sword down in a deadly stroke that sliced the man from shoulder to opposite hip. The peasant dropped his sword and staggered a couple of steps back, clutching at his belly in horror before collapsing to the hay-strewn floor. He twitched once then lay still, eyes open.

Momentarily stunned, Phoenix-the-boy surfaced and gulped. Nausea twisted his stomach. He'd killed someone. The third man rushed him with a wooden club and the Warrior took over again. He dodged instinctively, turning to chop at an exposed neck as the man stumbled past. He, too, fell to the haystrewn floor – and was clearly not going to get up.

Behind, he heard the hollow thwack of wood on skull,

followed by the thump of a large body hitting the ground. Sounded like Jade taking care of her adversary. He looked around. The smaller man had disappeared. A small, stifled shriek made him spin quickly, only to see the weaselly man standing next to Jade. His blade glinted at her throat. Wide eyed, she dropped her staff and put her hands up. Weasel-face grinned.

"That's the way, lassie. You too," he nodded pleasantly to Phoenix. "Put the sticker down or she dies."

Something in his voice told Phoenix the man was not joking.

"Do it," she whispered. "It's just money. We don't know what would happen if we get killed."

Phoenix hesitated. The game rules said they were supposed to have seven lives but did that apply now that they were actually in the game? It was only a Pre-release, after all. What would happen if they were killed here? Would their real bodies die in the real world? A cold sense of foreboding swept through his body, leaving him shaky. Slowly, he laid the sword down.

"Good choice. Now..." The thief sliced the leather tying Jade's money pouch to her belt and hefted the little bag in his hand. With a smile of satisfaction, he backed away. Phoenix watched with mounting anger. This was not how it was supposed to go. This was *his* game. *He* was the hero. He wasn't going to be beaten so easily by some grubby little git.

Perhaps seeing the red light of rage building in his face, the little man shook his head warningly. "Now then. I'm letting her live, aren't I? Surely her life is worth this little bundle." He tucked the bag into his belt, watching Phoenix as he edged away. "Besides, I can tell you what would happen if you got killed. You die. End of story."

Unable to contain the burning anger, Phoenix took a step forward. Jade cried a warning. The thief flipped the knife over, holding it by the blade as he retreated. Heedless,

Phoenix snatched up his sword and stalked after him. Their attacker slipped into the darkness with a grin. Phoenix growled, low in his throat, ran to the door and yelled after him.

"I'll get you, you coward!"

A faint laugh floated back through the night. The blade flew out of the gloom to bury itself deep into Phoenix's left shoulder. Staring numbly at the protruding handle, he turned towards Jade. She covered her mouth as if to stop a scream escaping. His shield slipped from a lax hand and clattered to the earthen floor. Pain exploded in his shoulder. He staggered back, astonished, groping for support. His heel caught in a loop of rope left on the floor. Jade screamed his name as he fell.

His head hit the packed earth. The world darkened and vanished.

****

CHAPTER FIVE

"Phoenix? Phoenix? Wake up, please?" Jade knelt anxiously over the fallen warrior, slapping his face lightly and experiencing a strong sense of déjà vu. Biting her lip, she frowned down at him. She had done her best. The knife was out, his wound healed to a faint scar. Why wouldn't he wake up? She didn't want to be left alone here. Night had fallen and the small barn jumped with shadows cast by the tiny, flickering candle lantern. It no longer seemed a safe, innocent haven in this bizarre world. Two of their attackers were definitely dead, the third probably as well. They had to leave.

She pushed open his coarse woollen shirt, searching for other wounds. Maybe she'd missed one. A glitter at his throat caught her eye and she gasped. Her necklace! She fumbled at her own neck, finding the slim chain she had clasped on only hours before. No, her teardrop amulet was still there. She tugged it out and craned her neck to stare at it; then looked closely at Phoenix's. It wasn't the same. In fact, they looked like two pieces of a puzzle – as if they should fit together. That made no sense! How could they even be here, in this reality? Why did he have one, too?

What did it mean?

Her sharp ears caught two voices at some distance outside: one light and familiar – the weasel-faced man who had stolen her purse - the other deeper and lower-pitched. She slipped to the door and peered out into the darkness. The rain eased and the cloudcover broke, allowing faint moonlight to illuminate the small courtyard between the inn and its outbuildings.

With her Elven eyesight, Jade could just make out what seemed to be three people: two larger men struggling together; a third, smaller figure, off to one side, watching. A knifeblade gleamed in the moonlight. What was happening? What if more thugs came? What was she supposed to do with Phoenix out cold?

Scuffled footfalls on wet earth were followed by a soft, muffled moan and the squishy thump of a body hitting slushy ground. One of the men was down. The other stood over him, hands on hips. He kicked the fallen figure. It didn't move. The smaller person sauntered forward, fingers reaching, perhaps for a pulse. There was some low-voiced conversation she couldn't quite make out. The taller man pointed back toward the barn before striding away into the Inn.

At that moment, Phoenix groaned, moving his head restlessly. Jade ran back to him, still casting quick looks at the door. His blue eyes opened and stared blankly at the thatched roof. Realisation flooded into his face and he sat up so fast he almost clashed heads with her. Pushing a long lock of hair back, he looked around in wide-eyed astonishment.

"It wasn't a dream! I'm still here!" He blinked at her then poked a finger at his shoulder, obviously relieved to find it undamaged. "Thanks."

She nodded absently. A new noise drew her attention. It was hard to tell what was going on but it sounded like something heavy being dragged toward the barn by someone who grunted a lot and slipped in the mud frequently.

"There's someone coming," she whispered.

He grimaced. "Man, what is this place, Grand Central Station? Where's my sword gone?" Clambering to his feet, he grabbed the weapon and faced the opening again. Jade picked up her staff, feeling sick at the memory of how easily she had cracked heads last time.

"Hello, the house!" A light, cheerful greeting floated through the door. It didn't sound like someone intent on attacking them. There were a few more grunts. The straining back and shoulders of a very grubby short person appeared in the half-lit entranceway. Whoever it was, they dragged the muddy and bloody remains of the weasel-faced man who had stolen Jade's purse moments before.

A few more feet and the newcomer dropped the body with an exaggerated sigh of relief. It flopped unpleasantly onto the floor. It was hard to tell through all the mud, but the carrier seemed to be a young boy. Turning to face them, he grinned impishly, showing two missing teeth. Jade relaxed a little. He didn't seem dangerous. He looked to be around ten years old; wiry but small for his age. His skin was sunburned nut brown and his sparkling brown eyes almost hidden behind a thick fringe of dark auburn hair. The much-patched homespun clothes he wore were two sizes too big and his feet were bare.

"You're the kitchen boy," Phoenix said, and she recognised the impudent youngster from the bar, earlier.

The boy grinned. "Sometimes." He held out a hand. Jade's purse lay on it.

She took it, hefting it as she eyed the boy. "Thankyou. What's your name?"

"Brynn the Leidyr," he replied with a quick bow.

Jade exchanged a glance with Phoenix, who smiled.

"Brynn the Thief, are you?" she returned wryly. "Is that why my purse is lighter now?"

The boy shrugged, quirking a grin. "Call it a fee for getting it back. Now…" He turned away and, began matter-of-factly searching the bodies.

Jade looked on in horrified astonishment. When he was done, Brynn hefted a reasonable dagger, a bronze bracelet and a few other small pieces, which he stored in apparently endless pockets. She snatched up her pack and cloak before he could rifle through them, too.

The boy reviewed the carnage they had created.

"You might want to find somewhere else to lay up for

the night, then get out of the village fast tomorrow." He picked up the small candle lantern and extracted the lit candle. Shadows jumped as the flame flickered in the breeze.

"Why?" Jade glanced around, bewildered.

Brynn tossed the candle into the nearest pile of dry hay.

"Because the barn is going to have an unfortunate accident and burn down." He pointed at the dead man he'd dragged in. "And because he's an informant for the Romans. He's already sent word to Londinium about you. Governor Agricola's Chief Comite will send troops. They'll be here by midmorning tomorrow."

Flames ate their way up the dry haystack toward the timber walls. Brynn strolled over and untied the cow, turning to lead her out of the barn. He paused, blinking at them in surprise.

"You're still here?"

"You killed that man and now you're burning down the barn to hide the bodies!" Jade blurted, overwhelmed by the speed with which events were unfolding.

He gave a one-shouldered shrug. "Actually, you killed those three and Llew, the innkeeper, killed the other guy. I just dragged the body in. If you're lucky, once the barn burns, the Romans will think two of them are you and stop chasing you. I don't like your chances, though. The Romans are pretty keen to be rid of your Folk."

"Her 'Folk'?" Phoenix voiced her next question for her.

Brynn tugged on the rope, towing the protesting cow past leaping flames. A chicken flew by, squawking indignantly. "Y Twlwyth Teg. You know." He frowned at their blank looks. "The Fair folk of the forests: elves, wood-nymphs and the like. The Romans hate you because you try to help our people against them."

"But..." Jade began then coughed as smoke billowed

up and flames began to take serious hold of the barn.

"Maybe we should talk about this somewhere else." Phoenix grabbed her arm and towed her outside.

Brynn slapped the cow on the rump. It mooed. Jade hurried to keep up. The boy seemed to be the only person who was willing and able to give them any sort of insight into this world.

When he turned around from tying the cow to a post behind the inn, Brynn saw them hovering and sighed. He cocked his head, put his hands on skinny hips and pursed his lips.

"Alright then. There's an abandoned house on the edge of the woods west of town. You can stay there tonight. You're obviously new to town, so I'll give you some tips." He cast a sly look from beneath long lashes. "For a fee, of course."

With the light of fire leaping behind and the sound of voices upraised in alarm close on their heels, Brynn led them silently through darkened fields, into the night. After close on half an hour, as far as Jade could tell, a dark, regular shape loomed. He slipped in and soon a faint, flickering light beckoned them to join him.

Jade entered and paused on the threshold. Although the farmhouse was obviously abandoned, someone had chosen to make it their home. Against one curved wall huddled a straw bed and a small fire crackled cheerfully in a central hearth. A few broken pieces of pottery and poorly-repaired chairs were a feeble attempt at home-making.

Phoenix opened his mouth to as though to comment. Jade elbowed him sharply. He shot her a frown then shut his mouth as she shook her head. For some reason, Brynn was living here, alone by the looks of it. It wouldn't be polite to say anything.

The boy waved them in. "Make yourself at home. I've got to go back and make sure Llew gets the fire out all right. I'll hoot like an owl when I return. Keep the door shut to hide the light." He vanished back into the darkness, leaving Jade and Phoenix to stare at the closed door.

Jade sank to the ground beside the fire, warming her chilled hands. After a moment, Phoenix did the same, his leather greaves and body armour creaking. They were silent for a while, numb more than relaxed.

Jade gathered her thoughts and asked the question uppermost on her mind.

"Do you think we'll be able to get home soon?" She said it now with little hope of a positive answer.

Phoenix shrugged, not seeming particularly concerned one way or the other. "Dunno. I don't know how we got here in the first place."

She pulled out the chain around her neck. "Maybe it has something to do with these. I noticed you've got one too and I remember thinking that weird lightning had somehow stabbed me right in the chest when it brought me here."

With a choked gasp, he tugged out his own and glared at her. "Where did you get that? It belonged to my father. It disappeared when he died three years ago."

Frightened by his anger, Jade hurriedly explained how she'd found it.

He frowned. "If that's true then you're probably right: somehow these amulets brought us into the game, which means we must need them to get back out. It just doesn't make sense, though."

"Which bit?" she said with heavy irony, "the fact that we were brought here by magic amulets or the fact that we're now inside the bloodthirsty sword-and-sorcery digital fantasy game we thought we were just playing for a bit of fun."

"Both, I suppose." He smiled, fingering the smooth face of his swordblade. "You have to admit it's more fun on the inside than the outside, though, huh?"

"You have a warped sense of fun." Jade grimaced,

going back to staring into the flames.

They sat in silence for a while, absorbed by the dancing orange lights.

Jade sat up straight, excited as a new possibility occurred to her. "Maybe could we contact other Players for help to get home?"

Phoenix narrowed his blue eyes then shook his head slowly. "Probably not a good idea. If you were an adult and a kid came to you with some story about kids being stuck in a computer game, would you believe them?"

She slumped again. "Guess not."

"Besides," he added, "I told you we're on our own for another couple of days. There aren't any other players here yet – not until the full release. Heck, we shouldn't even be able to see each other."

"So, what do we do?" She didn't expect any sort of useful answer out of him. He seemed determined to stay.

"Well…" He spread his hands. "We can make the best of it. Maybe we're here because we're supposed to play the game? Maybe that's the only way to get home."

"What?" Her voice came out as a strangled squeak. "All five levels? That's insane."

"Maybe it's just this one level," Phoenix said soothingly. "Maybe we just have to steal the Jewel of Asgard from Stonehenge – that's the task for Level One. Maybe once we do that and the full release is opened up we'll automatically go home."

"That's a whole lotta 'maybes'." She waved a hand back toward the village. "We nearly got killed in the first half hour of Level One! I've hardly ever played these things on the outside, let alone on the inside. There's no way I'm good enough to win one level, let alone five." She glared at him then pointed an accusing finger. "You just want to do it because you like computer games and you think this is fun."

Turning away from his guilty expression, she wrapped

her cloak around her body and stared moodily into the fire. She was tired, hungry and scared. There was no way she was going to play through the whole game to kill Feng Zhudai on the offchance it would take her home. Her limited Spellweaver skills would be hopelessly outmatched by the arch-wizard arch-badguy. There had to be another way.

Phoenix was silent awhile, poking a stick into the coals. "I suppose you're right. It's just…" He poked again, causing a shower of sparks to fly up, then sighed. "I'd really like to try, y'know? I hate my real life. This one might be…better."

"Better!" Jade gaped at him, appalled. "Getting attacked, stabbed, thieved and chased for weeks would be better? Man, your life must really suck."

He shrugged and there was a long, awkward silence.

"Besides," she added, trying another tack. "What's happening to the real us while we're in here trying to win? And what would happen if we lost all our lives? If this is the Pre-release version, do we even have seven lives? And we don't even know what this Jewel of Asgard is. How can we steal what we don't know anything about? There's just no chance. There's got to be another way to get home."

Even to her own ears, Jade sounded more and more like she was trying to convince herself. And she had a growing conviction Phoenix was probably right. In every book she'd read, the heroes had to complete their Quest. No matter how they tried to avoid it, they always ended up confronting the ultimate badguy in the end. This game was, after all, programmed by people who probably read the same books she did.

An owl hooted outside.

They both jumped. Phoenix laid his hand on his sword. The door opened just enough to admit Brynn's thin body. He slipped in and joined them by the fire. He reeked of smoke but he hadn't exactly been clean before anyway, so

Jade ignored it.

"Right," he said, pulling out a piece of what looked like beef jerky and gnawing on it. "Fire's out. Everyone's gone to bed. You're safe for the moment. So, here's the deal. You answer my questions, I answer yours. Yes?"

Jade glanced at Phoenix, who shrugged and nodded.

"Where are you from?" He waved the jerky around as though to indicate the world outside the hut. They both answered easily enough, using their avatar lives. He nodded, handing them some meat and indicating it was their turn to ask.

"Where's your family?" she asked, nibbling on the tough meat.

A shadow passed across his mobile face. "Killed by Romans three months ago. Where are you going next?"

Jade looked at Phoenix for guidance. "We're not sure. We're trying to get home but…it's complicated."

"So why do you want the Jewel of Asgard?" Brynn shot at them.

They gaped.

"How…?" she gasped.

Phoenix frowned and reached for his sword.

The boy edged away, hands sliding for his own dagger. "Don't get touchy. I heard some of your talk before I came in. You said something about stealing the Jewel. Why?"

"Why does it matter?" Phoenix returned.

Brynn eyed them, apparently assessing them in some way. He nodded once, as if he'd come to a decision.

"It matters because the Romans are after it, too. Word is that Governor Agricola's sent out a full cohort of men to get it. Apparently, whoever has the Jewel holds the key to ruling Albion. Agricola'll stop at nothing to get it. Since you're clearly not Romans, I'd rather you got it than him. If you want it, you'll have to move fast."

****

CHAPTER SIX

"It's pretty obvious we don't have a choice any more," Phoenix insisted. He had dragged Jade outside into the chilly night to discuss their situation away from Brynn's sharp ears. "If our only way home is by completing the quests then we have to get the Jewel before the Romans do."

"If," she hissed back at him. Her breath condensed into a cloud. "That's a big if. We haven't even looked for another way home."

"Come on Jade, seriously." Phoenix shook his head. "Do you really, truly believe there's an easy way out of this? Do you really think someone or something went to all the trouble to get us here, just to let us go for the asking? Face it, this is a game and we have to play our way out. Now we have a deadline, too. If we don't get the Jewel before the Romans, we really will be stuck here. Our only chance to get to Level Two – or home," he amended hastily as she turned a furious glare on him, "is to steal the Jewel from the Druids at Stonehenge. That's what the rules say."

"I don't know…" Jade began to pace, her outline dimly lit by the cloud-shrouded glow of an almost-full moon overhead. She wrung her hands together. "I just wish there was some way of knowing for sure what we have to do. A sign or something, to tell us we're on the right track. Then I would do whatever it takes…I guess."

Phoenix raised an eyebrow. She seemed more likely worry and think something to death, than actually do anything. He'd rather just get out there and get going. All this talking was giving him a headache.

He opened his mouth to say so, but she interrupted.

"Hey! Your pendant is glowing."

Startled, he looked down. There was a faint, purplish light glimmering through the thick wool of his shirt. He drew the necklace out, squinting down at it.

"Mine is too!" she added. "Maybe if we, like, fit them together like a puzzle and wish really hard, it will get us home."

Phoenix doubted it but he was willing to humour her if it would make her focus on playing out Level One. He unclasped his chain and they fitted the two halves together, holding them gingerly as though they were going to explode. He had a feeling it was going to take a lot more than wishing to get them home again and, to be honest, he didn't mind if they stayed awhile.

Nothing happened.

Jade sighed, her hopeful expression fading. "Well, it was worth a—"

A flash of purple-blue light seared their eyes, illuminating the astonished look on her face. It coalesced into a small, perfectly formed image that hovered in the darkness above the amulet like a hologram.

"Is that Stonehenge?" she whispered, sounding awed. It looked wrong, somehow. "Oh! All the stones are there. That's why it looks weird." She poked a finger through the translucent, compete stone circles.

The image vanished. She jerked her finger back.

Phoenix blinked, waiting for his eyes to readjust. The amulet under his fingers was warm. Catching Jade's eye he shrugged ruefully.

"You asked for a sign. I'd say that qualifies, wouldn't you?"

Her mouth moved but he couldn't hear any sound. A distant roaring surged into his mind, blotting out any words. Heat radiated from the amulets, still clasped in their joined fingers. He watched in horror as Jade's eyes rolled up in her head. Her knees gave way and she collapsed to the cold ground, dragging him with her. He couldn't release her hand or his amulet. Darkness claimed him – again.

This time it was different. This wasn't the brief darkness of unconsciousness. Phoenix opened his eyes to a gray, formless world of nothing. Beneath his body, the 'ground' felt soft but there was nothing to see; nothing with which to orientate himself or get a sense of 'up' and 'down'. Distance and time were meaningless. Gray encompassed all.

Without actually moving, he stood upright. Jade's hand was still clasped in his, their amulets still joined. He couldn't let go. Around their hands danced that same purple-blue light he'd come to associate with magic in the game-realm. So where were they now?

He glanced at Jade. She shook her head, her eyes both frightened and hopeful.

Home? she mouthed. He shrugged. Maybe she was right. Maybe this was some sort of between-world through which they could find their way home. He closed his eyes half-reluctantly. His visualisation of home wasn't particularly sharp or enthusiastic, so he wasn't surprised when the gray world was still there after he opened them. Jade's shoulders slumped.

A subconscious tension made him reach for his sword, only to find it missing. His dagger was gone, too. His curses fell silently into the absorbing, lightless world. He tried to wrench his hand free of Jade's but couldn't do that, either. Looking at her, Phoenix saw his own fear reflected in her eyes.

A gray-cloaked figure appeared, seeming to coalesce from within the featureless stuff surrounding them. Phoenix bunched up a fist, wondering if it would even connect here. Lean but stoop-shouldered, the figure radiated power. At the same time, it seemed forlorn and tired. The face lay shadowed in a deep cowl. Phoenix had the impression of age, pain and a hint of desperation.

We have only a few moments before I must return. I am

not strong enough for this any more. Thin and faintly amused, the voice sounded directly into Phoenix's head, bypassing his ears altogether. He blinked in surprise and felt Jade's clutch on his fingers tighten.

Who are you? Jade's thought-voice sounded much younger than her normal one. Phoenix wondered if it was her real-world voice he heard in his head.

The grey figure made a hasty movement as though rejecting her question. *The joining of your amulets gave me a small window of opportunity to speak with you but it will only work once. Do not waste time in useless questions. Listen.* When they did not interrupt, the voice continued. *You have been brought here to do what we cannot. You must stop Feng Zhudai. This world and your own depend on it. If you fail, both worlds are lost. If you fail, your otherworld bodies will die. If you fail, your lives there will be forfeit, and your world altered beyond comprehension. If Feng Zhudai succeeds in his ultimate plan, everything will change. Witness.*

With a wave of one knotted, white hand, images appeared directly in Phoenix's mind. He gasped in shock, clutching at his head with his free hand. It was like watching a montage of all the worst war films and horror movies. Half-disbelieving, he saw his school go up in flames; his house a tumbled ruin; his mother dragged, screaming into a small cell. On a broader scale he saw catastrophic wars across generations and continents. Ages of chaos and slavery. Above and beyond all, controlling the world like a puppeteer, hovered a shadowy figure in black. Somehow, he knew who it was – Feng Zhudai.

Abruptly, the scenes vanished, leaving red after-images dancing in the air.

They were still in the gray limbo world. The hooded figure before them drooped, as though drained of what little energy it had. Phoenix caught a glimpse of pale skin and a pain-pinched mouth.

I will return you to Albion. The first step you must take to stop Zhudai is to get the Jewel of Asgard before Agricola does. He will strike on the Equinox, when the Keepers of the Jewel are at their strongest and also at their weakest.

The Equinox! It was Jade's thought, and Phoenix heard the fear underscoring it. *But that's at least five or six days away. If Phoenix is right, we have less than two days before this whole game...world is overrun with more Players. That's not enough time. I just want to go home!*

The hint of a laugh brushed across his mind. *Time...time does not run as quickly at this end of the continuum. A day here is but a few hours in your world. You will have time, if you are wise. If you truly wish to go home, this is your only path.*

But we don't even know where the Jewel is! Jade's anguished wail interrupted.

Did you not see the stone temple, girl? That is where you will find the Jewel and its Keepers.

But...

No more questions. The figure flung up a trembling hand. *A journey of a thousand miles begins with a single step. You must get the Jewel first or Feng Zhudai will wrest it from the Romans and be strengthened by its power. With the Jewel in his hands, he will be almost unstoppable. He will lay waste to this world and yours.* The figure seemed to sigh. *Indeed, the home you knew will never have existed. Do not mistake. What you do here will affect your world as much as this one. This 'game' is nothing more than a portal through which you have been drawn. This world is real, in its own way. Let neither the Jewel nor your Amulets, nor lives fall into Zhudai's hands if you ever wish to return home. Protect the Jewel. Protect the Amulets. Stop Zhudai. You are our only hope now.*

Go.

The hand waved again. The gray world blinked out of existence.

Phoenix lay on the half-frozen ground, staring up at a million sparkling stars. He'd never seen so many stars. The Milky Way arced overhead in a glittering sweep of humbling distance and beauty. Beneath his fingers, lumps of cold, damp earth crumbled into its gritty components. It felt real. The stars looked real. Springtime scents and the first hint of dew on his skin seemed real.

Could it actually *be* real?

Images of destruction and despair flashed again behind his eyes. Could it be true? Could the game's arch-enemy actually destroy the real world? No. This was just a game. He was inside a game. A small part of his mind laughed, mocking his own thoughts. He believed he was part of a computer game but not that it was actually another world, as real as his own? Why believe one but not the other? They were equally outrageous ideas. There was certainly no technology in his own world that could put him inside a computer simulation like this. The only explanation was the magic of this one. Somehow, someone in this world had reached across time and space to pull him and Jade in.

Why them?

A groan broke into his thoughts. Beside him, Jade clambered to her feet, swaying as she brushed dirt off her cloak and breeches. She reached a hand down. He took it and hauled himself upright.

They stood in silence for a moment then she raised her head and stared about her like she saw the place afresh. A strange, unreadable expression flickered across her face. She turned huge, worried eyes on him.

"This is real?" Her strangled whisper was barely audible.

Phoenix got a tight grip on his own spiralling uncertainties and feigned a casual shrug. "Seems so. For a given value of 'real', I guess. Real enough, anyway. Who can tell? We don't know if that guy was telling the truth." He tried a grin, hoping it didn't look too stretched.

She managed a small, lopsided smile but he could tell her heart wasn't in it. Frowning, she slipped her necklace back on, turned and walked toward Brynn's little thatched house.

"I guess you're happy now," she muttered. "You get your wish to stay and play the game out."

Phoenix snorted, feeling his heartrate slow a little. "I wanted to play a game, not feel like the survival of the entire world rested on my shoulders. It wasn't supposed to turn out to be real – just a bit of fun." Lighthearted though his words were, their solidness settled uncomfortably in his guts. He'd wanted an escape from responsibility, yet here he was taking on more than ever.

When Jade didn't reply, he glanced across. Her smooth brow was marred by two deep, shadowed frown lines. "You ok?"

She flashed him a quick, haunted look. "I s'pose so. I guess I'm just trying to wrap my head around it. This means we do have to play this through. Of course, maybe we don't have to do all five levels. Maybe, if we stop Zhudai from getting the Jewel, that will be enough and we'll be sent home at the end of Level One. Oh, I don't know!" She paused, twisting her hands together again. "It just seems too hard. I just want to go home."

Phoenix didn't know what to say, so he wisely staying silent. He wanted to stay, even with the added responsibility. This was still way more exciting than homework and being grounded.

Finally, Jade sighed, flinging her arms wide. "Who was that, anyway? How do we know she wasn't just one of Feng Zhudai's minions? How do we know that this world will affect ours?"

"She?" He blinked in surprise.

"It was an old woman." Now it was her turn to look surprised. "Couldn't you tell?"

He shook his head. "Man, woman - whatever. The

point is: Zhudai's hardly going to send one of his own people to tell us to stop him at all costs, is he?"

"I suppose not." She made a frustrated noise and wrapped her arms across her chest. "I just don't know if I can do it! She said our real bodies will die if we fail? What if I can't handle it? What if I let you down? I can't save the world. I'm just a kid! I don't even know what to expect."

Phoenix shrugged. "Do you ever know? That's life, isn't it? If you knew everything in advance, it'd be pretty boring." He really didn't understand her. How could anyone function always worrying about what might happen? You just coped as things came up, didn't you? Learned as you went along. At least, that's what he did.

"But I'd be able to prepare for it; make plans; get ready." Her voice rose plaintively.

"Get a grip, Jade." He grabbed her arm, losing patience with her worrying. "This is only Level One. I'm sure we can handle it. Look how well you used your staff and healing powers. Just don't think about it so much. Use your character's skills and yours. All we have to do is get to Stonehenge and steal the Jewel before the Romans get it. Just focus on that."

The resigned, fretful expression on Jade's face showed she was far from happy with the situation. "But we don't know where we are; or where Stonehenge is from here; or what the Jewel itself is. How are we supposed to steal it? How do we find the Druids? How are we supposed to stop Feng Zhudai from capturing it, us, and our Amulets? We have to have some sort of plan."

"Well..." Phoenix grinned in the darkness. "There's a ready-made local guide and thief just sitting inside waiting for us. We could ask him for help? The rulebook did say we could each choose a Companion."

"But..." Jade stopped, staring at the closed door. "He's a kid and... a thief."

"He gave your purse back and he's helped us tonight,

hasn't he? Besides," he said, tasting a hint of his own bitterness, "I'd say he's grown up pretty fast as an orphan in this world. Let's go back inside see what he says, huh?"

****

CHAPTER SEVEN

"So, what do you say?" Phoenix held his fingers out to the fire and across glanced at Brynn. "Will you guide us? For a fee, of course." The grin he sent Jade was ironic. She frowned at him.

"To this 'Stonehenge' place," Brynn raised his eyebrows. "Well, normally I'd say 'yes' - especially to the fee." He flicked a cheeky grin at Phoenix. "I've worn out my welcome in this village. With the Romans coming tomorrow, it's time to move on anyway. The only problem is, I've never heard of 'Stonehenge'. Sorry."

Jade moved closer, deciding she'd have to get involved. She picked up a stick and began to draw in the packed earth floor. She drew a long, wiggly line and two dots. She pointed to one dot.

"This is Londinium." She looked at Brynn, who tilted his head to examine the drawing then nodded. "So, this is the River Thames." She indicated the wiggly line.

Brynn frowned then his face cleared to understanding. "Oh, the Plowonida, you mean. The 'wide river'. They only call it the Thames upstream, where it's narrower."

She pointed to the other dot. "This is where we need to go – Stonehenge. That's where the Jewel is."

The boy grinned. "You mean the Carega Amgarn. Why didn't you say so?"

"The 'Stone Circle'," Jade translated aloud. "Yeah, that must be it. Can you take us there?"

"Of course." Brynn nodded. "I went there two years ago, when we took my brother to join the Druids." He took the stick and drew another set of lines, one paralleling the river and another crossing it and turning south. "We won't be able to take the road for long, though. The main one along the river is patrolled by Romans. We'll have to go through the woods until we get to the ford. It'll mean going through the Dywyllwch Brennau."

He paused, looking straitly at the pair, clearly expecting a gasp of shock. It translated to 'Dark Woods' but must mean something far more sinister to him. When they just looked blank, he explained.

"The Forest Folk of Dywyllwch Brennau don't take kindly to intruders, what with the Romans chopping down their trees lately. They like to lead travellers astray with illusions and tricks. There are all sorts of nasties in the deepest parts. It won't be an easy passage."

"Of course it won't." Jade sighed, casting a resigned glance at Phoenix.

He grinned, patting his sword.

They set watches that night, at Jade's insistence. Their run-in with the local thieves made her skittish. Not that she slept much, anyway. Instead, she spent most of the night alternating between miserably missing her father and doing her best to understand the new body, memories and skills at her disposal. This was the adventure she had always read about; wished herself into. Now that it was really happening, she was terrified. It was all much harder, grubbier and nastier than she'd ever expected. She was stuck in a frightening, violent world and there seemed to be no way out, except to play the game through to the end – an end they now had to race the Romans to reach.

Finally, close to dawn, she fell into an uneasy sleep. Her last waking thought was that, if she were very lucky, this would all turn out to be a dream when she woke. Her sleep was haunted by knife-wielding peasants, grey-robed wizards and angry Roman soldiers.

In the morning, dawn revealed 80AD in all its unpleasant glory. Jade sat up and sighed, rubbing gritty eyes with dirty fingers. She felt filthy. Her hair and clothes smelled of smoke. Brynn laughed at her when she washed her face and hands in a bucket of freezing water drawn from the well. Shivering, she tried to pat her long, white-blonde hair back into some semblance of order. Eventually, she gave up and tied it back with a strip of leather, wishing for shampoo and a hot shower.

After a sketchy breakfast of some sort of thin gruel, they gathered their gear. Brynn cast one last look around his temporary home and shrugged. He carried a leather hunting sling and his pockets bulged with sling-stones and various small, probably-stolen artefacts. Otherwise, he took precious few things away with him, leaving most as though they didn't matter.

Brynn opened the door and they stepped out into a bright, spring dawn.

Phoenix blinked in the glare of the morning sun. Holding up a hand to shade his eyes, he leaned over and muttered in Jade's ear, "I suppose sunglasses would be too much to ask for?"

She screwed up her nose and pulled the hood of her cloak up to shade her eyes.

"Sunglasses, cars, microwaves, MacDonalds, toilets, showers, laundries and refrigerators – all too much to ask for."

He grinned and she couldn't help but smile back. This adventure seemed a whole lot less scary in the clear light of day.

Phoenix squared his broad shoulders, squinted down the road and raised his right foot. "Well, what was it the grey woman said? A journey of a thousand miles begins with a single step. So here we go." He put his foot down and Jade did the same, laughing.

Brynn shook his head, brushing past them, heading south. "Come on. If you want to stay ahead of the Romans, we'd better take more than one step. Oh." He paused, glancing back at Jade before pulling a small leather bag out of a pocket. Casually he tossed it to her. It clinked.

"Since you've hired me, I guess you'd better have your money back, so I can get paid."

Jade caught it, gaping at the boy. She snatched open her own purse and tipped it out onto the ground. Gravel poured forth, clattering into a small heap.

"You…you…" she stammered. "You stole all my money?"

Brynn shrugged, grinning. "Last night. I took it from the Roman snitch. I didn't think I'd ever see you again. It seemed like a good idea at the time." He cocked his head. "I am a thief, after all."

"How can we trust you?" She snapped her teeth shut and glared.

"I gave it back, didn't I?" he said simply. "Let's go. It's a good fifty leagues – close to a sevendays walk if we're not going to take the roads. We have to get to the forest as fast as we can. Keep a watch for patrols."

Without further explanation, he jogged away.

Jade looked at Phoenix, who grimaced and shrugged as well. "Like he said: he's a thief. Don't stress," he added, obviously seeing her annoyance. "We need him. If this Equinox thing is only a few days away, then we don't have time to find anyone else. We'll just keep an eye on him. Let's go."

He swung into a ground-eating easy jog and, shortly after, she caught him up, still frowning.

Soon, they'd left the tiny hamlet behind and followed a well-used road running alongside an expanse of marshy land that bordered the river. On their right were small fields, cattle and straggling stands of forest. Twice they jogged past carters carrying goods in the opposite direction, back toward the village they'd left.

They ran and walked alternately, mostly in silence except for the jingling of Phoenix's sword sheath. Jade's long fair hair escaped the tie and streamed out behind her in a light spring breeze. Birds twittered alarm calls in the forest as they passed and the sun rose warm in a clear blue sky. Their characters were used to this sort of travel and they barely had to breathe hard to keep up a steady pace.

They reached the edge of the farmed land and halted, staring at a vast, dark forest rising like a wall before them. The Roman road veered sharply left, skirting the edge of the forest as though frightened of the place. Traces of an older, less well-marked path ran straight ahead.

Brynn pointed. "We go in here. If we're lucky, we'll make it through without encountering the Forest Folk."

"I thought they'd be friendly to non-Romans," Jade said, brushing her fingers over the pointed tips of her half-Elven ears.

"Years ago, yes," Brynn shrugged. "But the Folk here have been long besieged by the Romans and no longer trust anyone." He glanced at Jade. "I'm not sure they would even welcome you, my lady, not being a full-blood Elf and all."

Jade looked at him, startled. Phoenix frowned at her. It hadn't occurred to either of them that her half-bloodedness might cause a problem with Elvenkind as well as the Romans.

Brynn set off and the two Players shouldered their packs once more, following him off the road and into the gloom of the forest.

*****

Under the canopy, Phoenix paused for a moment, listening to the soft sounds of the forest, letting his eyes adjust to the dappled light falling on the leaf-strewn floor. As they moved on, he soon realised that part of him was always watching and listening. His Warrior self was always alert. His brain seemed to know what woodland sounds it could safely ignore and what might pose a threat. His eyes flicked to follow small movements and his hand never strayed far from the hilt of his sword. His feet involuntarily picked out the smoothest path and made little noise. It was quite incredible to feel so at home in the forest when he'd never spent any time here in the real world. Phoenix grinned to himself, feeling the flow of energy and the flex of muscle in his body. He could get used to this. This was definitely more fun than just watching on the computer screen.

They ran and walked through the forest for an hour, heading steadily west and slightly south, paralleling the Roman road. With casual skill, Brynn brought down some small game with his sling in preparation for dinner, later. Twice they stopped and hid to avoid being seen by travellers on the nearby road. A third time they lay, breathless, while a small contingent of Roman soldiers, their scarlet-plumed helmets bobbing in time, marched toward the capital.

Back on the forest path, Phoenix noticed a growing discomfort and finally decided he couldn't wait any longer. He stepped off the track and stopped, dropping his pack on the ground.

"What's up?" Jade asked.

"I have to go," he muttered.

Brynn nodded, understanding immediately.

Jade glanced around, looking perplexed. "Go where?"

Phoenix looked at her steadily for a moment then jerked his head toward a cluster of large shrubs a little way inside the forest.

"I have to *go*," he said significantly.

Jade stared at him for a moment then her eyes lit with understanding and she giggled. Brynn grinned, too.

"I get it. Well, I have to admit…" She looked around. "Going to the toilet isn't usually mentioned in the books I've read. You'd better grab some leaves." She smiled, adding in a whispered aside, "They don't invent toilet paper for a couple of thousand years."

Phoenix flushed with embarrassment and ripped three of the largest leaves he could find off a low plant that grew amongst grass and pretty spring flowers, beside the track. They were a bit too crinkly to be really useful but they were the best he could see.

"I wouldn't use that if I were you," Jade warned.

Brynn's smile widened. "Ah milady, you're a better person than I. I wouldn't have told him."

"We can't afford him to be ill," she pointed out.

Phoenix looked at the leaves in his hand. They looked ok. "Why can't I use these?"

"It's Ragwort," she replied. "Toxic. You can absorb the poison through your skin and it can lead to breathing problems." She indicated another plant not far away. "Try that one. It's harmless. Nice big leaves, too."

Phoenix glanced at her and back at the leaves in his hand. Was she just pulling his leg? He decided not to risk it. She might be a bit of a worry-wart but she seemed to be confident enough about this. He tossed the leaves away and murmured a self-conscious thanks. Ignoring Brynn's laughing comment that he should just wash his backside in a stream like the everyone else, he grabbed the other leaves and walked purposefully off into the forest, trying to look cool about what he was doing.

He wasn't. He'd never considered that toilets, as he knew them, didn't exist in this time. It would be at least eighteen hundred years before the first indoor flush toilet was invented. Right now, a hole in the ground was the best anyone could expect. Being out in the forest meant he couldn't even have that. Resignedly, Phoenix ducked behind the bushes and hoped they were thick enough to screen him from Jade's eyes.

Minutes later, feeling much better, he emerged from the bushes, found the forest path again and glanced around for the others.

The path was empty.

His companions had vanished.

****

CHAPTER EIGHT

Phoenix's first instinct was to yell their names. He even opened his mouth but then his Warrior awareness kicked in and he shut his teeth with a snap. A rapid scan of the dirt path showed no extra footprints and no signs of a struggle. His backpack was gone, too. So, they were either hiding for some strange reason, or they'd gone ahead without him – which seemed unlikely.

A flash of scarlet off toward the road caught his eye. Romans! A small sling-stone whistled past Phoenix's ear. Jade hissed at him from several metres away. Silently, he slid over to join them where they hid behind a large thicket.

"Romans," Brynn murmured, pointing toward the road. Phoenix nodded. This group of soldiers moved slower than the others. There were more of them, too and they weren't sticking to the road. Several men fanned out on either side and crept through the forest, swords drawn.

"They're looking for someone but it's not us," Jade whispered. "I guess I speak Latin, too," she added with a shrug when Phoenix looked a question at her. He realised then that he, too, understood the low conversations drifting toward them.

Brynn nodded in agreement. "I can't hear who it is, but they want him pretty badly. They have orders to take him straight back to the Governor in Londinium." The boy shivered, clutching his thin shoulders. "Wouldn't want to be that guy. Let's get deeper into the woods. The Romans probably won't come too much further in." He tugged at Jade's sleeve. She nodded and slipped in behind his small figure.

Phoenix glanced once more at the nearest soldiers. He felt strangely reluctant to run away. It felt wrong to his

Warrior self. He should be out fighting the Romans, not skulking away like a coward. No, they only had a few days to get the Jewel and thwart both Feng Zhudai and the Romans. No time for fun. Sighing with regret, he got a grip on himself and followed the other two deeper into the green gloom.

They didn't risk another path for a long while. Even when they found one that seemed to lead in the right direction, they were wary and tense. There was little speech between them and no thought of stopping to rest or go to the toilet. Some of the excitement had worn off the day. There was more than a hint of danger in the air.

Ahead, Jade drew her cloak tighter about her slender form and peered into the forest.

"What's wrong?" Phoenix whispered.

"I feel…" She glanced around again. "Like someone's watching us."

Phoenix felt it too: a strange prickling on the back of his neck. There was someone – or something – watching them. Had the Romans found them? Surely they wouldn't just watch - they'd charge in and capture by force of numbers. Not the Romans then. So who? Brynn's Forest Folk?

From the corner of his eye, he caught a glimpse of movement.

"On the left," he murmured. Jade and Brynn nodded in silent agreement. Brynn slipped his sling from his pocket and casually loaded a stone into it. Jade held her staff in both hands. Phoenix loosened his sword in its sheath. They padded on, deeper into the woods.

Moments later came a cry of shock and pain from somewhere off to their left. It was followed by a strange creaking, like the timbers of an old house settling at night; then the sound of a blade chopping into wood. More creaking. A human voice cried out again, this time a call for help. The three companions stopped, exchanging wary looks. The yell became more desperate; the creaking louder. Jade chewed on a fingertip and took a step toward it.

Brynn grabbed her arm. "He's speaking in the Roman tongue. It's a trap, my lady. Don't go."

"Why would they bother with a trap? They have hundreds of soldiers." She shook off his grip. "No, that's someone in trouble. Come on, Phoenix. Please?"

Phoenix nodded, sword-hand itching. "Suits me. Whoever it is, we need to shut him up anyway, before he draws every soldier for three miles around."

Together, the Players pushed through a screen of bushes. Behind them Brynn swore then caught up, sling ready.

Jade pulled up short at the sight beyond. In the centre of a large clearing stood a massive tree, its canopy of small, dark green leaves reaching at least ten metres in every direction, its trunk a thick and ancient tangle of ropy aerial roots bound together. She frowned.

"This is wrong," she said. "It's a strangler fig. They only grow in the tropics of Southeast Asia, not here."

"Don't forget where 'here' is at the moment," Phoenix reminded her, "the programmers can put anything they want anywhere they want, remember?"

There was a gasp from Brynn, who had just appeared at his side. The boy raised a shaky finger. "Look."

They followed his finger and saw a young man, about their own age, entangled in the dangling roots of the tree. They were wrapped around his limbs and torso from ankle to neck. Beneath him lay a sword, with which he must have been hacking at the plant. It had fallen from a now-limp hand. His face was dark red, his eyes closing as he gasped for breath.

"How…" Jade began.

"It's a Strangler," Brynn said. "They catch their prey this way. He's done for."

"Not if I have anything to do with it." Phoenix grinned, snatching his sword out and striding forward. Three swift slices detached the roots encircling the boy's neck. They swung uncontrollably through the air as though lost. The stranger gasped, blood draining from his face as breath returned. He began to struggle again. Phoenix waded in, hewing at the thicker vines twisted around his torso. Every time his sword bit into wood, reddish sap oozed out like congealing blood. A thin, high-pitched screeling echoed in the clearing. Jade clapped her hands over her ears.

Dozens more ropy vines dropped down from above, lashing wildly about, stretching toward Phoenix and the tree's victim. Phoenix yelled as one connected and tightened around his ankle. It yanked. He slashed at it as he fell, freeing his foot just as he hit the ground. Winded, he staggered upright, panting for breath. The stranger was once more cocooned and suffocating. Phoenix raised his sword, hacking again and again at the branches.

"Wait!" Jade screamed, her hands pressed to the side of her head. "Wait! You're hurting it!"

"That's the idea! It's killing him!" he shouted back.

Jade ran forward, grabbing his sword arm. "Wait. Please. Let me talk to it."

A thrashing root reached for her. Phoenix severed it in one clean blow. She winced.

"Please," she begged him. "I can make it stop. I know I can. Brynn, give me that rabbit you hunted earlier."

Phoenix glanced at the entangled stranger. His eyes were closed again, his movements feeble.

"You'd better be right and make it fast or he'll be dead in a few seconds." He backed away, out of reach of the seeking tendrils.

Jade dropped her staff and stepped into them, holding the rabbit in one hand. The tree tendrils shivered, reaching for her like a thousand thin fingers. Brynn cried a warning. Phoenix held him back as he tried to rush to her rescue. She closed her eyes and let the tree encompass her completely.

There was silence in the clearing. Breathless moments passed. Phoenix cursed his own stupidity. It wasn't going to work. Now both of them were caught and he couldn't chop them free fast enough. Growling, he raised his sword again and took a step toward Jade's swathed shape.

Abruptly, the branches and roots fell away, vanishing up into the canopy and into the ground. Jade stepped free unharmed, like a magician's assistant revealed after a trick. Her hands were now empty. The stranger collapsed unconscious to the ground. She ran to his side, pulling out her herb bag. Laying hands on his chest and head, she closed her eyes. A purplish haze shimmered around her hands as she Healed him.

He sucked a deep breath, his eyes flying open to fix on her face. Remembered horror dawned and he sat up, staring at the now-dormant tree towering overhead.

"It's ok," Jade assured him. "It won't hurt us now. I gave it some food and asked it not to."

He stared at her, lingering pain in his eyes. "You…you…asked it?"

She nodded. "But I think we should leave its territory. Phoenix did hurt it and it's not very happy with us. Can you get up?" She rose, staggering, a hand to her head as if in pain.

The stranger nodded. Scrambling to his feet, he put an arm around her waist, steadying her until she could walk. Then he picked up a bow and quiverful of arrows from the ground nearby, regathered his sword and held it tightly, glancing again at the quiescent tree as they moved far out of its reach.

"You alright?" Phoenix asked Jade as the two approached.

She nodded. "Just a difficult Healing. He had broken ribs and a collapsed lung. It took a lot of energy. We should keep moving, though. That made a lot of noise. It might bring the Romans straight to us if we stay."

"Ha! Too late," Brynn spat, "he is a Roman. See?" He pointed at the distinctive gladius sword in the young man's hand. "A soldier, I'd say. It was a trap and he's the bait. His cohort will be here soon."

Phoenix raised his own weapon, eyeing the newcomer warily. This boy-man was strong-looking but Phoenix thought he could probably take him in a fair fight. They would be close-matched. He seemed to be about sixteen years old but carried himself confidently, like someone older. He was almost as tall as Phoenix, with short, black hair and a long, straight nose. His eyes were dark in a strikingly handsome face. His short tunic and cloak were plain but of good cloth and well made. A heavy gold ring glinted on the little finger of his left hand.

Jade laid a hand on the Brynn's shoulder and held him still. She retrieved her quarterstaff but didn't raise it. Tilting her head, she seemed to assess the stranger.

"You're Roman but you're not a soldier, are you? Who are you?"

"No, I'm not yet a soldier, my lady." The stranger bowed gracefully.

There was an air of calm resolution about him, now that danger was past. His face was composed, eyes steady. He sat down on a fallen log and drew a long, slow breath. It was not the action of a man about to attack them so the others slowly lowered their weapons.

"But I am the son of a Roman soldier." He held up a hand as Brynn muttered under his breath. "I am no threat to you, though. Indeed, I would call you friend, for you are my enemy's enemy."

"What does that mean?" Phoenix asked. "Which enemy? We're starting a collection."

"I have forsworn my Roman heritage," the stranger replied with dignity.

He gazed into the distance for a second, a brief look of

pain on his handsome features. There was a short, awkward silence. He seemed to be the sort of person who spoke little and thought long and hard before he did.

"I don't like what it means to be Roman in the land of the Bretons. We slaughter all who resist us and kill the Fair Folk, like you my lady, for no reason except that we are frightened of them." He glanced at them. "It's wrong and I won't be part of it."

The tension drained from all three companions as they sensed his honesty.

Phoenix sheathed his sword and reached down a hand. "We should keep moving. What's your name?"

"Marcus," came the answer as the boy gripped his hand and pulled himself upright. "Yours?"

"I'm Phoenix, this is Jade and Brynn." He indicated the others.

"I'm indebted to you all for a timely rescue." Marcus bowed. "Especially you, my lady."

Jade blushed and smiled faintly at him. Brynn glowered.

They moved off through the greenwood, putting distance rapidly between themselves and the uncanny tree.

As they walked, Marcus looked at each in turn. "An odd group. A Breton warrior with a Greek name, an Elven woman walking abroad in daylight and a child. Are you pledge-partners and this your son?" He jerked his head at Brynn.

Phoenix started and almost laughed at the thought. He hid the laugh with a cough, realising it would be hard to explain that he was actually only thirteen years old and could hardly be the father of a ten year old! He kept forgetting this body was more like eighteen. He exchanged a glance with Jade, who gave an embarrassed half-laugh and shook her head as she too must have realised what he meant by 'pledge-partners'.

Phoenix tried to look cool but probably only succeeded

in looking flustered. "No, we're not…um…together." He was never going to hook up with anyone. "Brynn, we met by chance. He's our guide."

After a few moments of uncomfortable silence, Marcus took up the conversation where he had left off. "So, if you're not married, why do you carry matching blades?" He nodded toward at the knife Phoenix carried in his belt.

Phoenix swapped startled looks with Jade. She snatched her own knife from her belt and examined it. He moved over and held his beside hers. Marcus was right. They weren't identical – Jade's was bronze rather than iron - but both knives were decorated in a similar way. Phoenix touched a finger to each of the seven small rubies embedded in the hilt of her knife and in his. They glowed faintly.

Jade whispered, plainly not wanting the others to overhear. "The rules did say we have seven lives in the game? Could these show how many lives we have?"

Phoenix turned his knife over. "I don't know but the old woman in the gray place said that if we failed we'd die in our world, too. If these are extra lives, at least we have some chance of succeeding."

"Seven isn't very many when you consider what we're up against," she shot back.

She was right. Seven lives didn't seem like much when they had five levels of the game to complete. It was a frightening thought and Phoenix saw the fear in her eyes again. There were so many dangers in this world and they knew so little. He'd been an idiot to remind her.

He looked up to see Marcus and Brynn watching them. Acting casual, like it was nothing important, he muttered, "Let's work it out later," and moved away. He needed time to think. That was hard to do with Marcus and Brynn watching his every move.

It was a relief when the Roman boy asked a different question. "Where are you going?"

Phoenix hesitated. They didn't know this guy. He said he was an enemy of Rome but could they believe him? He might be a spy. On the other hand, how could the Romans possibly know they were even in the forest to be spied on? He compromised, giving a part-answer.

"We're following the river for a while. Heading west. You? Are you the one the Romans were looking for today?"

He nodded. "I escaped from an encampment just over the hill yesterday morning. My father sent men after me. I've been keeping only just ahead of them. I don't know these woods and I'm afraid I'll stumble straight onto the Legion if I keep going in circles. That's why I was following you. You seemed to know where you were going."

"And now?" Phoenix prompted. "We're heading deep into the woods. Brynn here knows the paths but we don't and you don't. Where are you going to go now?"

Marcus scanned their faces as though wanting to ask an important question but afraid the answer mightn't be what he wanted. "Honestly, I was hoping I could travel with you for a while. At least until we're out of these woods and away from my father's men."

Phoenix glanced at Jade. She raised one eyebrow and held up two fingers as if to say – Companion number two? He twisted his mouth. He wasn't sure about this guy. They were already a walking target with Jade being a half-elf and therefore wanted by the Romans. If they added a runaway soldier's son to their group, wouldn't it be even harder to evade the troops?

"We'll definitely meet more Romans on this trip." He watched the Roman boy's handsome face. "Are you able and willing to kill them if you need to? I won't let them take us and I won't risk Jade's life or Brynn's to rescue you if you get captured."

Marcus held his gaze for a few moments. He pulled his

bow off his shoulder. Nocking an arrow to the string, he drew and released it in one smooth movement. The arrow flew through the gloom and thunked into a tree trunk over thirty metres away.

"Able, yes, willing, definitely," he said grimly. "I don't want to see the Fair Folk destroyed either." He bowed toward Jade.

She blushed again and glanced away.

Phoenix looked sceptically at the arrow. It wasn't too hard to hit a tree. The shot wasn't a great indication of his skill as an archer. Even as he opened his mouth to say so, Brynn gasped and ran forward. He jerked the arrow out with an effort. Something small and dark fell to the ground. Brynn picked it up gingerly and brought it and the arrow back. He dropped the dark thing into Phoenix's palm and handed the arrow back to Marcus with a look of reluctant respect.

In Phoenix's hand lay a large, grey-brown moth. He glanced again at the tree it had been on. O...K..., he was willing to concede that hitting a camouflaged moth at that distance in the uncertain light under the canopy was pretty darned good shooting. Phoenix caught Jade's eye and she nodded slightly. Brynn screwed up his mouth and nodded his agreement.

"Very well," Phoenix said, "you're welcome to join our odd little group as long as you like but I warn you, it's not looking like an easy trip. Hope you're prepared for the worst."

Marcus grimaced. "What could be worse than that tree-thing?"

Brynn sent him a knowing look. "That was nothing compared to what else lives in this forest, Roman."

****

CHAPTER NINE

Dusk swept in and they had managed to elude the Roman trackers all day. Phoenix was conscious that they hadn't made great time in the forest and was all for pushing on into the night. Since Jade was the only one with decent night vision, however, he finally agreed to stop after twice tripping over branches and roots sticking out onto the path.

They searched for a suitable, hidden campsite. Two huge fallen logs served well, once they'd laid leafy branches between as a makeshift roof. Marcus made a small, hot fire from wood gathered close by. They screened it carefully on all sides with stones and branches so the glow couldn't be seen at a distance. Brynn and Jade found a few herbs and early forest foods while Phoenix plucked and gutted a pheasant Brynn had brought down with his sling, earlier. He skewered it on a green stick and began to turn the spitted bird above the fire.

After they ate, there wasn't much left to do except sleep and they were all tired enough to do that easily. Phoenix opted to take first watch. Marcus volunteered to take second, Brynn third and Jade the last. Phoenix resolved to stay awake through Marcus's watch, just in case. He kind of trusted the young Breton boy not to murder them but trusting a Roman seemed stupid. It wouldn't hurt to keep a close eye on him for a while, anyway.

Seeing the others settled, Phoenix wrapped himself in his cloak and sat with his back to the fire. Peering into the chill darkness, he hoped nothing would emerge to attack them. They were deep in the Forest but had yet to see evidence of Brynn's mysterious Forest Folk. The feeling of being watched had not gone away, though. He still had the urge to look over his shoulder; still felt the uneasy sensation of being followed.

Marcus's eyes had not been the only ones on them.

Fortunately, the cool spring night passed without incident. Each watch reported no trouble and the weary travellers rested well. At the first light of pre-dawn, Jade woke them, telling Phoenix she wanted get an early start. He grumbled a little but couldn't really argue when she pointed out the time-deadline facing them. He ran his fingers through matted hair and watched her touch Marcus on the shoulder. Marcus sat straight up, his eyes wide and a small knife in his hand. He murmured an apology and, without explanation, tucked the knife into a sheath strapped to his calf. Jade stared at him, pale and shaken. Phoenix frowned. What made him so jumpy?

Brynn bounced straight up without complaint. He disappeared for a few minutes, returning with a handful of pheasant eggs and mushrooms. Jade inspected the fungi and pronounced them safe to eat before cooking them in her little pot into a sort of messy scrambled eggs.

With a full stomach and a good night's sleep, Phoenix hoped they'd cover more ground today. They'd lost a lot of time avoiding the Romans, rescuing Marcus and taking devious paths through the woods yesterday. They still had over a hundred kilometres - forty-five leagues - to cover. Going through the rough paths of the forest and fields would probably take them four more days at least – if they didn't encounter anything unexpected. The Equinox was only about five days away, by Jade's Elven calculations. Any delays on the road could be disastrous.

The morning went quite smoothly. So smoothly that even Jade looked more relaxed. The weather held cool and clear. For almost two hours Brynn led them through the Dark Woods without incident. By mutual consent, they worked their way closer to the road again – out of the deepest, creepiest part of the woods. For the most part, their path was easy – almost boring - through the dappled, cool green.

Lacking other distractions, Brynn and Marcus began a competition to see who the best marksman was. After Brynn brought down two pigeons and Marcus a hare and a pheasant, Jade called a halt to their fun.

"At this rate, you'll waste all your ammunition and we'll have more food than we can possibly carry or eat," she said. "Have some sense, would you both?"

Brynn grinned and handed Phoenix a bird to carry. "With two big tough Warriors to feed, I don't think that's possible." He ducked when Phoenix reached out to slap him lightly across the head.

Marcus said nothing. He drew himself up and bowed his head in stiff acknowledgement of the reproof. Jade flushed as he turned his back and followed Brynn along the path.

Phoenix tried hard not to feel glad that Jade had criticised the Roman. It bothered him that he was a little jealous of Marcus. The boy had a cool, quietly-confident sort of attitude that irritated Phoenix for no reason he could think of – except that it made him feel somehow inadequate. He hated that. He'd started this game so he could feel better about himself, not worse. Unsettled, Phoenix padded along in the rear, trying to work out what was annoying him. Finally, he realised - he wanted some action again, not all this walking.

A short while later, they stopped for a brief rest. They ate in silence, drinking from waterskins and nibbling journey bread Jade produced from her pack. A sense of nervous anticipation pervaded the group and discouraged idle conversation. There were few animal noises – as though the weight of expectation muffled all sound. The sensation of being watched grew again. Around them, the forest seemed to close in: trees loomed larger; the canopy denser. Phoenix kept catching flickers of movement at the edge of his vision, only to see nothing when he turned his head.

At last, none of them could stand it any longer. Brynn was the first to jump to his feet, ready to continue. In hushed tones, Jade reminded him to be on the lookout for a stream so they could refill their waterskins. The boy waved a hand over his shoulder in acknowledgement as he headed off again.

With Brynn and Marcus in the lead, they stepped into a sunny clearing and headed for a small stream meandering through the middle. Phoenix and Jade joined them, blinking and half-blinded in the light after hours in the shade.

"Take them!" A hoarse shout rang out.

All four dropped their waterskins and snatched at weapons. Phoenix stood beside Jade and faced their enemies, his heart racing at the thought of battle. Marcus had an arrow in his bow so fast it looked like magic. Brynn held his sling at the ready, eyes darting around the clearing. Eight Roman soldiers stepped into the sunlight, surrounding them on three sides; swords drawn and faces wary. A ninth man joined them. He wore a short red cloak flung back over one shoulder and carried a staff in his right hand. His armour was of chainmail and his helm bore a crest of stiff red horsehair. An officer.

Phoenix glanced at Marcus, wondering if it was his father but the boy kept his weapon ready and didn't speak. If anything, his face was even more calm and set. Phoenix tossed up his options and decided to try and settle things peacefully. Action was all well and good but his aikido sensei would be horrified if he didn't at least try to talk his way out of it.

Raising his left hand, palm open, he tried to sound confident. "We are travellers. We've done nothing wrong. You're making a mistake."

The Roman leader smiled knowingly. "I think not. Governor Agricola himself is after this lad." He pointed with his sword at Marcus.

Phoenix suppressed a groan. He knew it had been a mistake to include Marcus.

The officer pointed at him. "You, I believe, are wanted for killing a Roman soldier two days ago and for murdering four villagers that same night. And of course," the officer added softly, "the Governor will pay handsomely for you." He indicated Jade and smirked. "A good catch, I'd say. Now put down your weapons and let's go."

There was a soft twang. Marcus's arrow flew from his fingers. It embedded deeply in the right shoulder of the officer, just where the armour was weakest. The officer swore, shouting for his men to advance. Marcus's hands blurred as he nocked and shot arrow after arrow with deadly accuracy. One by one, soldiers fell back, clutching at shafts protruding from their bodies.

A loud clang and a groan told Phoenix that Brynn had entered the fray, gleefully slinging rocks. Although every instinct screamed at him to jump into battle, Phoenix had to wait until the soldiers were closer before he could fight. There was no point getting in the way of Marcus's arrows. The Roman was doing a pretty good job of holding the soldiers back on his own.

Even as that thought crossed his mind, Phoenix spotted movement in the forest. Marcus shouted a warning and Brynn groaned. Sixteen more soldiers stepped into the clearing. They held up long, curved rectangular shields, making them almost invulnerable to arrows and stones alike. Marcus dropped his bow and yanked out his sword. Brynn pulled out his little knife, looking frightened but determined. Whiteknuckled, Jade held her quarterstaff ready. Phoenix renewed his grip on his sword and grinned fiercely. Here it came.

With angry mutterings, the Romans advanced step by step toward the four. Several of the soldiers Marcus had injured were back on their feet and had joined their comrades. Four lay sprawled, lifeless on the ground. The officer was no longer smiling. They meant business.

The closest soldier reached Phoenix and jabbed at him with a gladius. Phoenix parried awkwardly and stepped aside. Again, he experienced that frightening moment of total confusion as his two selves tried to react in their own fighting styles. His real-world self reacted with aikido - turning, blocking, redirecting. His warrior-self from this world tried to chop and slice. This time it was worse. It paralysed him; froze his mind and body with conflicting messages. He would be killed if he didn't act.

A second soldier closed, and a third. Phoenix stopped thinking. He deliberately blocked out his thirteen-year-old mind and let his sword-fighting memories flood in. Those muscle-memories were stronger in this form. It was his only hope. His body, trained and ready, reacted faster than he could think anyway. He spun, lashed out, connected with a sickening sound, danced out of the way, spun again, parried and jumped back. His dagger was now in his left hand, ready to stab or deflect blows. There was no time to unsling the shield from his back. Another clang of sword on sword; a slash underneath, into unprotected ribs. He backed away, breathing hard, trying to block out the screams of the wounded. Three men down.

Fighting against the Romans was unlike fighting the untrained peasants or the native bandit-warriors of this land. The Romans used a sword designed for both hacking and thrusting. Phoenix's sword and style were based on chopping. He found it hard to avoid and block the quick, jabbing thrusts.

More soldiers approached. The only thing the Phoenix and his friends had to their advantage was that the men couldn't come at them in large groups without hitting each other. He risked a quick glance and saw two soldiers at Marcus's feet, groaning. Three were unconscious near Jade, either from her quarterstaff or from Brynn's darting knife.

It was hard to tell. Her staff dealt multiple resounding blows on any man stupid enough to come within reach.

He'd looked away too long and barely managed to avoid being skewered through the stomach. The blade grazed his hip and he yelled in pain and shock. Anger flowed through him, giving him new power. He was strong. He could beat these idiots easily. There was no way he was going to be defeated on Level One.

Twist, cut; turn; parry; stab, slice.

Two more Romans down but still more came on. Phoenix's breath rasped fast and hard in his throat. He gave ground under a furious assault by two determined soldiers. His little group was slowly but surely, pushed back until they were almost standing in the small stream. The ground was slippery with mud and moss. It grew harder to keep his footing and there was less room to manoeuvre.

A shrill scream rent the air. Phoenix risked a glance back to see Brynn held tightly by the Roman officer. The boy bit and kicked for all he was worth, but Phoenix could see it was no good. The Roman produced a dagger and held it to Brynn's throat.

"Put down your weapons or I'll kill him!" The officer shouted above the melee.

Helpless frustration replaced anger in Phoenix's veins, turning his resolve to despair. They couldn't lose the game so soon. It just wasn't fair. For a brief instant, he considered letting the officer simply kill Brynn. After all, Brynn and the officer were both just digital constructs in the game. But he couldn't. Not only did it go completely against his nature and training but what if the cloaked old woman was right and this world was real in some way? Then wasn't Brynn real as well?

With a growl of confusion and annoyance, Phoenix lowered his sword. Immediately, three soldiers placed the tips of theirs at his throat. The same happened to Marcus and Jade when they followed his lead. The officer smiled thinly and relaxed his grip on Brynn. Holding the boy by the elbow, he shouldered his way through the soldiers.

Phoenix looked bleakly at him through half-closed eyes, wondering what would happen now. He supposed their group would be split up. Marcus would be dragged back to his father; Brynn sold into slavery; Jade tortured and killed and himself forcibly recruited into the Roman army, at least.

There seemed to be nothing he could do about it. No. There had to be something. The game just couldn't end here. There had to be a way to win.

Warmth pooled on his chest. The amulet. It was heating up again. What could it mean? He couldn't risk looking down at it. There were still three swords at his throat.

Just beside him, he heard Jade's voice murmuring something in Elvish. The Roman Officer looked startled then frightened. He switched his knifepoint from Brynn's throat to hers.

"Shut up, woman, or I'll shut you up permanently."

From the corner of his eye, Phoenix saw Jade gulp. She had raised her hands when a soldier had taken her staff. They were held at about shoulder height, palms out to show she was weaponless. She'd stopped speaking but her fingertips glowed with a faint purplish haze. Hope surged. Did she have a trick up her sleeve that could get them out of this helpless situation?

He tensed every muscle, waiting for a chance to act if she did.

****

CHAPTER TEN

"Sneeze!?" Phoenix stared at Jade in disbelief. He couldn't decide whether to laugh or slap her back in congratulations. "You've got this cool magic to use and you get your enemies to sneeze?" All around them, Roman soldiers convulsed and fell over, unable to keep their feet or see straight.

"Well?" Jade sent him a hurt look. "It worked didn't it?" She waved a hand around the clearing, indicating the twenty or so soldiers collapsing as wave after wave of sneezes shook them.

Phoenix gazed at them then gave way to the relieved laughter bubbling inside him. Jade's frown changed to a reluctant smile. Marcus and Brynn exchanged amazed looks then Brynn, too, howled with laughter. Marcus permitted himself a small smile, though his eyes were troubled.

It took several seconds before they were in control enough to gather their weapons and gear again. Ignoring the Centurion officer, who staggered after them swearing, sneezing and feebly waving his sword, the four companions filled their water skins at the stream and wove their way through the shuddering soldiers toward the other side of the clearing. A final glance showed the men looking truly miserable. They certainly weren't capable to retaking their prisoners.

Still chuckling, Phoenix wiped his eyes. He noticed Brynn snatch up a woven bag one of the soldiers had dropped at the edge of the clearing. Catching the boy's bold gaze, Phoenix frowned then shrugged. It might contain something useful and they could use all the help they could get at this point. Brynn grinned and flipped the sack over his shoulder with a jaunty whistle.

A sharp pain in his side made Phoenix wince. He touched his hip gingerly and felt a shallow slice there, bleeding sluggishly. There wasn't much he could do now. They had to get back into the forest and away from these soldiers. Gritting his teeth, he followed the others.

"Let's get out of here before it wears off," he ordered, limping into line behind Jade. The sounds of wild sneezing faded and the group became more serious again as the gloom deepened beneath the green canopy.

"So how long does that spell last?" he asked.

"About an hour." She shrugged.

Phoenix grunted and nodded to Brynn to pick up the pace a bit. They had to get somewhere safe for the night before the soldiers found their trail again. The cover of darkness was still a few hours away.

"Why not something a bit more permanent, like 'disappear' or 'die' or 'explode'?" Phoenix gave voice to the question that had been nagging him for the last ten minutes. Marcus nodded and Brynn dropped back, evidently wanting to know the answer as well.

Jade, who seemed to be lost in thought, frowned before answering. "It has to be a single word imperative verb that they are capable of performing," she replied at last.

He blinked at her. "In stupid-people speak, please."

"Oh. Sorry. I was thinking of something else. The spell is limited," she explained, "You can only use one word. It has to be an order to do something, but it has to be something they're actually able to do." She raised her eyebrows at Phoenix who nodded, doubtfully. "You can't order someone to explode because they're not physically capable to doing that. So I'd pour all my energy into the spell and it would just suck me dry trying to achieve what I'd asked. The person wouldn't explode but I'd die."

"Ah," Phoenix said, understanding. "So, you've got a few more useful words up your sleeve, I hope. I mean," he added wryly, "sneezing isn't exactly the most awe-inspiring way of defeating our enemies."

Jade pursed her lips. "It was all I could think of at the time. I'd be happy to hear any better suggestions. Anyway…" There was a hint of hurt in her voice again. "My sister gets hayfever with massive sneezing fits. She says it's like your brains explode out through your nose and get replaced by snot. She can't think clearly all day. I'm sure it will keep the soldiers off our trail for long enough." Apparently satisfied that she'd explained herself, she glanced around the forest with a frown. "Can you guys hear something? Like a voice, whispering?"

When the others shook their heads, she frowned again and chewed on her lip, sinking back into whatever had been preoccupying her before.

Phoenix exchanged rueful glances with Brynn and gestured for him to continue leading the way.

They walked well into the evening without stopping again to eat or rest. Twice Brynn led them up streams to cover their tracks and once they hopped for several hundred metres across an area of exposed boulders and logs. At one point, they came to a fork in the path. Both ways were indistinct. Brynn hesitated.

"Go right." Jade's voice and expression were somewhat dreamy.

"You sure?" Phoenix glanced around. The forest looked the same in both directions but, as far as he could tell, going right would take them more north than west. It would also lead further into the deep woods – further into Fair Folk territory. Somehow, they'd been lucky enough to pass unnoticed through their land so far. Was it worth pushing their luck?

Jade blinked slowly at him then shook her head as though to free it of fog. She was her normal self when she replied. "We'll be safe. We're being watched but we won't be harmed."

"How do you know?" He gripped his sword, not liking the thought that they were still being watched.

"I…" She shrugged. "I just do. You'll have to trust me on this one."

Unsatisfactory as that answer was, Phoenix had to accept it. She was, after all, an Elf and therefore attuned to all things natural. If this was a Forest Folk haven, it made sense her character would feel bound to it.

Still, it made him uneasy.

In the end, it was so dark that they all had to rely on Jade's night vision to guide them. It annoyed Phoenix to feel so dependent on anyone but they needed to put some distance between them and the Romans before they could camp for the night. Finally, she stopped and told them to wait. Phoenix stood in the gloom with Marcus and Brynn, feeling stupid. When she whispered in his ear, he almost yelled in shock.

"There's a small cave just a little way up this hill. It's off the path and hidden behind a stand of trees. We should be able to light a fire." She took his hand. He groped for Brynn and the boy snatched Marcus's hand. Jade guided them through the blackness, murmuring soft instructions about where to put their feet.

When they reached the cave, Phoenix dropped his pack and shield with relief. Jade and Brynn gathered wood near the cave entrance and started a small fire, well hidden by piled up rocks and a thicket of trees outside.

Marcus began to gut and pluck the pheasant he'd caught. Phoenix skinned a hare, although he had to suppress the urge to chuck. Luckily his character knew how to do this stuff, because he'd certainly never had to do anything like it in the real world. Chopping up dead animals was the last thing he wanted to do. His hip ached and so did his sword arm. They were all exhausted but he refused to be the one to admit it. Technically, he was older and stronger than all the others. If they could keep going, so could he.

Brynn tended the fire as Marcus added bits of meat into a pot of boiling water. Jade tossed in some wild onion and herbs and the stew began to smell appetising. Phoenix finished cleaning and butchering the hare and pigeons. After a moment of thought, he rigged a drying rack above the fire and hung the strips of meat up. With luck, in the morning, they would be smoked enough to keep the next day. He could finish cooking them the next night.

At last he sat back down and stared blankly into the leaping flames. Listening to Jade bemoan their lack of bowls and spoons, Phoenix was reminded of the woven bag Brynn had collected from the soldiers. Maybe there were spoons in it. Or maybe treasure.

"Let's see what we have here then." He picked up the bag and tipped it out on the dirt floor. Brynn protested that it was his bag but subsided when Phoenix glared at him. There wasn't all that much of interest as far as he could tell, anyway. There were two spoons and two small wooden bowls, a loaf of flat bread, a little sack of dried leaves, a long coil of thin rope and another bag – made of some shiny black material. Jade pounced on the bowls then examined the dried leaves, declaring them to be bay leaves – native to Greece. She put one into the stew and tucked the rest into her backpack for use in seasoning food. The bread went into their foodstores. She passed the rope to Marcus. He wrapped it around his waist like a belt, saying it might be useful sometime.

Phoenix picked up the black bag and turned it over in his hands. It only weighed nothing and felt slippery, cool and decidedly empty. The bag itself wasn't huge but the drawstring mouth seemed enormous and the red cords holding it shut were very long. It looked as though the bag could be opened right up to lay flat on the ground. Curious, he tried it.

He tugged the mouth open as far as it would go then

spread it out on the ground. Sure enough, it formed an almost perfect circle about a metre across. He reached out to smooth the black material flat but Brynn snatched at his hand.

"Don't touch it!" the boy exclaimed, wide eyed with wonder.

"Why? Do you know what it is?" Phoenix drew his hand back.

"I think it's a Hyllion Bagia," Brynn breathed. "A magic bag made of cave-spider silk. They're really, really rare and really really valuable." His eyes sparkled with interest, greed and a hint of fear.

"That doesn't help me much," Phoenix grumbled.

He searched his character's memories but his Warrior hadn't come into contact with much magic in his short life. The ancient Brittonic words Hyllion Bagia translated literally as 'all I bag', which didn't make a great deal of sense. Frowning, he tried to remember what little he'd read about magical items in the game rulebook but nothing helpful leapt to mind. He glanced at Marcus, who shook his head to indicate his ignorance.

Jade knelt beside Brynn and examined the bag without touching it, her head tilted to one side. "I can kind of see the magic shimmering around it like a sort of purple-blue glow," she said, narrowing her eyes.

Phoenix stared at it hard but it only shimmered when his eyes began to water. "So, what does it do?"

"Well..." Brynn picked up a small stone and held it over the open bag. "This."

He dropped the stone onto the black opening.

The stone vanished.

Jade gasped. Phoenix reached out but yanked his arm back just in time. If the stone had disappeared, what would happen to his arm if he touched the material?

"Where did it go?" she breathed.

Phoenix reached out to her. "Hold my hand. I'm going

to find out."

"No." Marcus laid a hand on his shoulder. When he turned angrily on the Roman, Marcus just tightened his grip and shook his head. "I'm the least valuable member. Brynn's your guide. Jade's a Spellweaver and a woman. You're their leader. I should be the one to try it out."

"But—" Jade protested.

"No, Jade," Marcus said gently. "I…we don't want to risk losing yo…anyone." The Roman boy caught Phoenix's astonished look and turned away, flushing red.

Jade looked annoyed, confused, then quietly pleased.

"Nobody needs to go," Brynn interrupted. They all looked at him. "It's just a Hold-all. You put stuff in and you take it back out again when you need it. It never gets heavier so you can put as much as you like into it."

Phoenix eyed the empty blackness dubiously. "But how do you get it back out again?"

Brynn swallowed and bravely reached into the bag. His arm disappeared up to the elbow. Jade choked a warning and Marcus turned a few shades paler.

"Stone," the boy murmured then withdrew his hand. There, in his palm, was the small stone he'd cast in moments before.

"So, you have to name what it is you want before it will come out?" Jade asked.

"As far as I've heard, that's the way it works." Brynn nodded. His usual, cocky expression was back now he'd shown them, without mishap, how the bag worked.

"But what if there's lots of stuff in there already?" Phoenix was troubled. Who knew what the Romans had already stashed in there.

Brynn shrugged. "Unless you know what it is, it's staying in there." He screwed up his nose and added, "but I suppose you could guess and fish around a few times. These bags are supposed to be harmless."

Phoenix glanced at Marcus. "What do you think the

Romans would have stored in here?"

Marcus crouched beside him and gazed into the black hole for a long moment. Shaking his head, he replied thoughtfully, "I'm finding it hard to believe they even had one. We…" He stopped then started again. "They don't really believe in this sort of magic."

"What do you mean 'this sort of magic'?" Jade demanded. "Do they believe in some sort?"

Marcus nodded slowly. "The Gods have a magic of their own. They use it to help or hinder mortals when they feel like interfering in our lives. Romans don't believe in…er…Earth-magic or magic items, like this."

"'Earth-magic'?" she prompted.

The Roman looked uncomfortable, glancing at Jade then away again. "The sort that you practice – using plants and the like. The sort that comes from being close to the land; part of the land – like Elves are." He seemed to feel he'd said enough and sat back to tend the stew.

Phoenix raised an eyebrow at Jade. "Shall we give it a go?"

"Nothing to lose, I suppose," she replied dubiously.

"Except maybe an arm," quipped Brynn.

Phoenix glared. The boy grinned back irrepressibly.

Gingerly, Phoenix inserted his right hand into the bag. There was a strange, tingly-coldness as his fingers disappeared. He wriggled them and waved his hand around but encountered nothing. Thinking, he said aloud,

"Knife." Nothing. "Bread." Nothing. "Helmet." Still nothing.

"Let me try," Jade reached her hand in. "Hat." Nothing. "Shoes." Nothing. "Cheese."

Phoenix stared at her. "Cheese?"

Brynn snickered.

She shrugged. "Just a thought."

He studied the size of the opening, wondering what a Roman would fit through it that might be useful. Mentally, he pictured the Romans as he'd seen them in the clearing. They'd looked pretty much like every picture of Roman soldiers he'd ever seen. Armour made of small plates of metal covering their chests. Metal helmets. Short leather and iron skirt-things. Sandals. Short swords. Big shields. What was missing?

"Try 'pilum'," Marcus suggested.

"What?" Phoenix frowned. "What's that?"

"A spear the infantry carry," he replied.

"Yes!" Phoenix slapped his own thigh. "That's what was missing." He put his hand back in. "Pilum."

Thump. Something wooden and heavy slammed into his hand. His fingers closed around it automatically and he drew it out…and out…and out. The spear was so long that he had to turn it to point out the cave's entrance. The iron tip scraped the roof.

They all stared at the long wooden shaft and the thin metal length and tip, then back at the small black bag in astonishment.

"I wonder how many are in there," Jade breathed.

"There are eighty men in a Centuria," Marcus said. "It's possible the Centurion officer was using the bag to carry the pila for all his men."

"You mean there might be seventy-nine more in that little bag?" Phoenix said.

Marcus looked thoughtful. "Personally, I think it would be impractical to have eighty men all trying to get their weapons out of one small bag. It's more likely that he only used it to carry his own possessions or maybe the pila of his own Contubernium." Seeing their blank looks, he explained. "A Contubernium is eight men; a Centuria is ten lots of Contubernia."

Phoenix did the mental calculation then shook himself.

"So, basically…" His heart sank even as he spoke. "We've now got the Centurion's personal magic bag, probably full of his own personal items."

"Probably," Marcus agreed. He thought for a moment, and then added, "You could try asking for Roman coins, too."

With a portentous feeling, Phoenix plunged his hand back in and said, "Roman coins."

Instantly, his hand was full of what felt like money. He drew them out and dribbled the silver coins onto the ground. Brynn pounced on them. Marcus picked one up and nodded.

"Roman coins - denarii," he confirmed. "Either the Centurion's own hoard or the pay for his men."

"Well, I did forget to bring any with me," Phoenix grinned weakly at Jade.

"Oh no." Jade stared at the little pile of coins Brynn was counting. "We've beaten their soldiers, stolen their money and they know about Marcus and me." She bit her lip. "I'm afraid we've just given eighty soldiers a really good reason to keep chasing us."

Marcus grimaced. "I hate to say it but it's not going to be just one Centuria of eighty men any more. They...don't like to be humiliated. It's more likely to be the entire Cohort they belong to." He returned their horrified stares stoically. "Four hundred and eighty soldiers will be after us now."

****

CHAPTER ELEVEN

Nobody but Brynn got much sleep that night. After they ate, they put the pilum, most of the money plus a few of their own things into the Hyllion Bagia. Jade tended to their various, luckily slight, injuries. Then they briefly discussed their travel plans for the next day. But as that primarily consisted of more walking through the forest and avoiding Romans, there wasn't much to say. So, Marcus added a little wood to the fire and Jade took first watch while the rest settled down to sleep as best they could.

Phoenix found that the slightest noise outside the cave brought everyone except Brynn full wakefulness each time. The youngster slept blissfully on until Phoenix woke him for last watch. Their skittishness was wasted. The half-expected horde of Romans did not appear.

Day dawned and with it came a change in weather. Clear conditions were replaced by a constant, chilly drizzle that soaked through the thickest cloak. Overcast skies meant the weary adventurers slept later than they should have. It was well past dawn when they emerged from the cave ready to move.

Following Brynn, they returned to the trail. Rain dripped ceaselessly from shiny leaves. Underfoot, wet leaves and mud stuck to their boots, sandals and bare feet. They left a clear trail but it was difficult not to. The air was cool enough that noses turned red and fingers stiffened with cold.

They ate as they walked. Breakfast was a sketchy affair of bread and a few pieces of hare and pheasant meat from the night before. Phoenix chewed the cold fare, disliking it but wishing there was more. What he would give for a hot plate of bacon, eggs and toast right now. Or even a carrot. Not broccoli, though. Not even a year in this time would make him want broccoli. He wondered if they even had carrots and broccoli in ancient England. Jade would probably know.

He'd been gone from home for three nights and two days. This was the third day. It seemed like much longer. Some of the initial excitement of being in the game had worn off. The rain certainly wasn't helping. He didn't remember rain being a normal part of any other game he'd played. He sighed, kicking at a wet mushroom growing beside the path. It disintegrated in a satisfying way.

They were still several days away from Stonehenge and each moment they delayed made it more likely the Romans would get the Jewel first. He wasn't yet ready to face the possibility of failing. This world was still a heck of a lot more interesting than his own but he was beginning to miss a few things about home: toilet paper and soft beds being high on the list.

"Do you think we'll make it home?"

Phoenix started. Jade walked next to him, looking miserable and bedraggled.

"What?" He wasn't certain he'd heard her words and not just his own thoughts.

"I said: do you think we'll make it home?" she repeated.

Shrugging, he jammed cold hands under his cloak. "Sure, if we can beat the Romans to the Jewel."

"I miss my family," she said forlornly. "This is a lot harder than I expected. I'm…scared we won't even make it through Level One."

For some reason, her low mood annoyed Phoenix. It coincided too closely with the niggling doubts he was trying hard to ignore.

"Don't be stupid." He spoke more harshly than he intended. "Of course we'll get home. Besides, I thought you were starting to like it here." Looking at Marcus's broad back ahead of them, he added, "Or at least like some of the people here."

Jade's pale face flushed and she wrapped her cloak about her body. She sent him a quick, hurt look before hurrying ahead to walk beside Marcus.

Phoenix mentally kicked himself. He hadn't meant to take out his own bad mood on her. He was just as unsure as she was but felt like he wasn't allowed to show it. The success of this mission seemed to rest totally on his shoulders. It was too much. He had no idea how they were supposed to keep avoiding the Romans; no idea how to find the Jewel of Asgard and no idea how to steal it, even if they could find it.

Being in the game was a lot harder than just watching it on a flat screen.

He was responsible not just for his life but for three other people's as well. It was fine to say that, logically, Marcus and Brynn were not real people but what if they were real? They felt real. He was sure that if they got injured or killed, it would hurt to see.

He let out an angry, wordless growl and ripped a small branch off a tree. Hurling it into the undergrowth, he waved away the questioning looks of the others and kept walking. He didn't want to be responsible for anyone else. He didn't want to even think about it. This was a game. It was meant to be fun. He just wanted some good fights and a bit of a lark. He didn't want it to be real. Reality sucked.

*****

Jade strode ahead, hurt by Phoenix's unfair comments. Whatever was bugging him, he had no right to take it out on her. They were all tired and worried. She brushed away tears and sniffed defiantly. She would not cry.

Being the youngest of seven had long ago taught her that sulking didn't do any good – nobody paid attention – so Jade deliberately pushed her hurt feelings aside. She caught up with Marcus. Stealing a quick look up at his handsome profile, she found herself thinking about Phoenix's comment. Did she 'like' Marcus?

"Is something bothering you?"

She looked up at him, startled. Had he somehow read her mind? No. He was referring to her spat with Phoenix.

"Oh." She tried to sound relaxed. "I didn't sleep well – kept thinking I heard someone calling my name - and Phoenix is just being grumpy."

"What did he say to you?"

Jade opened her mouth then blushed. "Nothing important," she finished lamely. "Can I ask you something?" It seemed safer to change the subject. Marcus nodded. "Why did you pull a knife out when I woke you yesterday morning? Were you expecting to be killed in your sleep?" she asked jokingly.

Marcus stared at her gravely for so long that Jade felt the smile slip off her face.

"You mean you were expecting us to murder you?" She wasn't sure how to feel about that. Kind of sickened and a little upset.

He made a gesture as if to brush away her words. "No, no, not you," he assured her then added, "It's just a habit."

"You have a habit of expecting people to kill you in your sleep?" That was even more astonishing, if possible. "What sort of family do you have?" She was outraged on his behalf.

The Roman stared silently ahead for a few moments, his eyes on the path. Just when she thought he wasn't going to answer, he spoke.

"My father's a soldier. You learn to expect violent death when you're brought up in a military family."

"Your father's death, maybe," she scoffed, "but surely not your own. You're just a ki…" she broke off, thinking about her history lessons. In olden times, when people didn't live very long, someone Marcus's age would be considered a man, not a kid. It was only in modern times that teenagers were thought to be too young for responsibility and treated like children. Marcus, by ancient Roman standards, was an adult.

It was a sobering thought. He was probably the most qualified of any of them to lead this expedition but Phoenix seemed to resent him. Jade was aware that Phoenix didn't quite trust Marcus but she did. She knew the Roman was hiding something but he had no evil intentions toward them – she could tell that instinctively. Anyway, they all had something to hide.

"I'm old enough to join the Legion." Marcus jerked his chin up.

Jade laid her hand on his arm and caught his affronted gaze. "I'm sorry. That was rude." She eyed him, remembering something else. "I've been meaning to say thank you for helping us." When he looked surprised, she continued. "You fought against your own countrymen yesterday. It must have been difficult for you. You barely know us and you've probably grown up with some of them. So, thank you."

Marcus touched her fingers lightly then dropped his arm away and grimaced. "It was no hardship to fight against that Centuria. It's well known their Centurion reports directly to Feng Zhudai."

Jade stopped in the middle of the path, her mouth open. Phoenix, who had been walking close behind, ploughed into her, sending them both stumbling. He apologised but Jade barely heard him. She grabbed his arm, her nails digging in.

"Marcus. Say that again – about the Centurion we fought yesterday. Tell Phoenix."

Phoenix looked back and forth between the two of them, clearly confused.

Marcus raised his eyebrows but repeated what he'd said. "I said that I didn't mind shooting the officer we fought yesterday, since he's in league with the Governor's chief advisor, Feng Zhudai."

Phoenix took an involuntary step back as he heard the name. Jade met his startled look and didn't protest when he dragged her off to one side and hissed in her ear.

"But this is only Level One. What's the big Badguy doing here? He's supposed to be with the Emperor Han Zhangdi and General Ban Chao in China, not with Governor Agricola of Roman Britain. I thought we wouldn't have to defeat him until Level Five!"

"I don't know," she replied in an undertone. "I was hoping you might. Didn't you say you'd read the rulebook? I only skimmed the startup information." She watched him rub his forehead as if he could squeeze the information out of his head.

He shook himself.

"I'm not certain of anything anymore," he admitted, "but I am sure the goal of the game is to ultimately defeat Zhudai in the last level of the game, not the first. Here, we just have to focus on getting the Jewel before the Romans do, so we can get to Level Two."

"Get home," she corrected.

Phoenix shrugged. "Whatever. Hey!" He raised excited eyes to hers. "Maybe if we kill Zhudai now, we can finish it here on this level and you'll get home sooner."

He must have read the doubt on her face, for he quickly added, "It's worth a try, isn't it?"

"I don't know," she murmured. "Zhudai is supposed to be some sort of super-wizard."

"Well, maybe in this level he's not so tough." He wrapped his fingers lovingly around the hilt of his sword.

"The only problem is…" She nibbled at her lower lip, trying hard to ignore a rising wave of panic. "We're not so tough in this level, either."

"True." His agreement seemed reluctant. "Well, maybe you'd better talk to Marcus and find out all he knows about Zhudai. It is a bit annoying that he's here."

"Annoying?" Jade blinked at him. "That's an understatement and a half."

She signalled Brynn to keep walking and turned back to Marcus. "So, tell me about the Governor's advisor. How long has he been in that position? What's he like? Where's he from?"

Marcus frowned. "There's little to tell." He spread his hands wide. "He arrived from Rome a year ago, sent by Caesar himself to help the Governor subdue the Celtic tribes. He's from some distant land, that I know."

"How do you know?" she demanded.

Marcus's dark eyes turned thoughtful. "Zhudai is a man like no other I've seen. His eyes are black and narrow and kind of…." He put his fingers at the corners of his own eyes and pulled them sideways.

Jade nodded. "He's Chinese."

"Chinese?"

Had the Romans ever traded directly with the Chinese in 80AD? She couldn't recall, so she just flapped her hands for him to go on.

"Never mind. Just tell me everything you know about him. Like how he helps the Governor. Is he just giving the Governor advice on battle tactics? What?"

Marcus talked and Jade listened, with Phoenix edging ever closer to try and hear, too.

Feng Zhudai had arrived from nowhere a year before to 'advise' Agricola on how to handle the rebellious Celtic tribes stubbornly resisting Roman rule throughout Britain. The methods he advised, however, were less than honourable and many soldiers resented the influence the foreigner had over their Governor. Marcus spoke darkly of mass slaughters of druids and disappearances of both local people and soldiers who spoke out against Zhudai. There was, apparently, a newly-constructed stone temple of sorts in Londinium. A temple solely for his use. A temple where people went in but never came out.

Marcus described him as 'cold' and somehow all-knowing. It was said that he could read the minds of anyone brought before him, could spy on people from a distance. There was even one story of a man who, after being touched on the head by the Chief Advisor, died moments later in hideous agony – but without a single mark on his body.

Jade listened in growing horror, occasionally breaking in with a question but somehow not doubting Marcus's tale at all. After all, Feng Zhudai had been programmed to be the arch-nemesis of the 80AD game. It made sense that he would be extremely powerful and totally ruthless. Unfortunately, knowing he'd just been written evil didn't make her feel any better.

Marcus fell silent at last.

"And the Governor?" she prompted. "Is he under some sort of spell or does he really trust Zhudai?"

Marcus laughed bitterly. "The Governor trusts no-one." He paused, looking thoughtful. "But it is possible that Zhudai could have some sort of arcane influence over him. That could explain why…" He broke off, fingering a long, still-pink scar on his forearm. "It doesn't matter. The point is that Zhudai is, somehow, controlling Governor Agricola. I would give a lot to put an end to that situation. Before he arrived, the Governor was at least willing to listen to reason about his treatment of the Bretons and the faery folk. It was only after Zhudai arrived that the Governor ordered the persecution of your kind and the wholesale slaughter of Druids, Bretons and Celts."

The Roman lifted his head and gazed at Jade, his mouth pressed into a tight line. "I fear my presence is severely endangering your life."

Jade frowned but shook her head. "It's alright. We know the soldiers want you back but you're the son of a soldier, so I doubt they'll actually try to kill us while you're with us. So really, you're probably keeping us safe."

"No." He shook his head. "It's not just because of who I am. The Romans are after me because I attempted to assassinate Feng Zhudai. The Governor is furious with me." Marcus looked straitly at Jade. "Since we saw that Centurion, I've known he has sent Zhudai himself to find me. The Governor wants me back, it's true; but Zhudai wants me dead."

****

CHAPTER TWELVE

"Oh, no!" Jade groaned. She sank down onto a log and dropped her head into her hands with a sigh. "So now we've got Zhudai after us already as well as half the Roman army? This is not what I was expecting when I started this."

Marcus crouched before her, his eyes troubled. "I'm sorry I have placed you all in greater danger. I should leave."

"No!" Jade grabbed his arm. "Don't go! I'm just overreacting. We'll…we'll cope."

He looked at her for a long moment then nodded slowly. She blushed and released him. Her heart thudded uncomfortably as he stood and faced Phoenix.

"What about you? Do I stay with you or go?" the Roman boy asked with quiet pride. "I know you have some mission to achieve and I don't want to jeopardise that or your lives with my presence. It's your decision."

Jade jumped to her feet. "It's all of our decision, not just Phoenix's. We're in this together." She stared defiantly at the two warriors, annoyed at Marcus's automatic assumption that Phoenix was leader, just because he was a boy. She looked at Phoenix. "But I don't think Brynn and Marcus can make a decision without knowing more. We need to tell them."

Phoenix stared at her, obviously caught off-guard. "Tell them what, exactly?"

"I think if we tell them what our ultimate aim is then Marcus and Brynn can decide for themselves if they want to help or not," she said uncertainly. "It's not fair to drag them around the countryside without knowing what they're getting into."

"Sounds like great advice to me," Brynn said. "I always like to know what I'm getting myself into - especially if it involves being killed by four hundred and eighty Roman soldiers and a mad foreign wizard." He held up his hands in surrender when Phoenix scowled at him. "Hey," he said, "I only signed on to guide you to Carega Amgarn and maybe help you steal the Jewel of Asgard and nab some treasure for myself. If there's more to this, it'd be nice to know now."

"Fine, then." Phoenix scrubbed a hand over his face, as though the last three days had finally caught up to him.

Jade could almost feel his exhaustion and impatience. He just wanted to get on with it. He probably thought she was making things more complicated than they needed to be.

"We're here on...a great quest." He seemed to be struggling to put it into words. Jade kept quiet with an effort as he continued. "We have to complete five tasks in five different parts of the world. The first is to get the Jewel from the Druids at Carega Amgarn, as you mentioned, Brynn. If we manage that and the other four lev...tasks then we should be able to achieve our ultimate goal - to kill Feng Zhudai."

Brynn's jaw dropped. Marcus frowned. Jade watched them both anxiously.

"But such tasks could take years," Marcus noted. "It takes many weeks to get just from here to Rome. Why should you have to travel all around the world to defeat Zhudai when he is already here?"

"Well, I'm fairly sure we won't have to travel overland to get to our next destination. The ga..." Phoenix stopped, glanced at Jade then began again. "Jade has a way of getting us to the next place by magic."

"There are only three of you." Marcus glanced at each in turn. "How are one warrior, a boy and a mere woman going to defeat Feng Zhudai?"

"Hey!" Brynn scowled and Jade had to press her lips firmly together to stop herself from echoing his outrage - 'mere woman' indeed.

Marcus flushed and bowed toward them. "I apologise. In Roman society children and women are not expected to go into battle. Please remember: I have seen what Feng Zhudai can do and, although you are both skilled, you cannot defeat him."

Phoenix grimaced. "To be honest, we weren't expecting him to be here. We are supposed to complete four other tasks before even meeting him. Doing them is meant to give us enough skills and strength to face him and have a chance of killing him."

"So, if you meet him in battle now you will lose?" Marcus stated.

Phoenix shrugged.

Jade nodded. "Probably."

There was a long silence as the four companions thought and waited.

"So, what do you want to do?" Jade finally asked. "We'd totally understand if you decided it was too risky to travel with us." She laid a hand on Brynn's shoulder and smiled down at him. "You can just take some of that money and go, if you want."

The boy gave a one-shouldered shrug. "I've got nothing more to lose. Zhudai himself ordered my family's execution and watched them die." His young face was grim. "I'd be perfectly happy to wander around the world for years if we could kill him in the end. I'm with you all the way. Besides," he added slyly, "I've always wanted to travel."

Jade exchanged a shocked look with Phoenix. She glanced at Marcus, wondering how he would take this latest revelation. Marcus's air of hesitation left him. He straightened, took a firm grip on the hilt of his sword and pulled it from its sheath.

Kneeling on the damp earth in front of Jade and Phoenix, he laid his sword at their feet and bowed his head. "I swear fealty to you both." He looked up, into their eyes, his expression earnest and determined. "My sword is yours. My life is yours. I will do anything in my power to help you achieve your goal for it is mine, also."

Phoenix put a hand on his shoulder. "There's no need for that, Marcus. We aren't your masters, we're your friends."

Marcus stood and sheathed his sword. He bowed. "Thank you for your trust, I know it wasn't easy to give. Still," he added, "I'm sure you would feel better if you allowed me to swear an oath – or if we all took an oath to each other, perhaps?"

"Er…?" Phoenix looked at Jade.

She grimaced and glanced around. Inspiration hit and she dashed a few steps off the path, returning moments later with her hands full of vines.

"Everyone put your left hand into the middle, palm upwards," she ordered. "If you're truly willing to be part of this group, that is. You don't have to."

After a moment's hesitation, they all did so. Using her right hand, Jade twined the vine around and around all of their arms, binding them loosely together in a green-and-flesh knot. Tucking the ends in, she instructed them all to lay their hands atop each other's, palm up. Then she fussed for a second, arranging their hands so that each palm was squarely on top of the last in a stack of hands – Phoenix's on the bottom, hers on the top. Next, she picked up a small amount of mud from the wet, puddled path and rubbed it into the middle of her palm.

"Er…Jade?" Phoenix asked, looking like he thought she was insane. Nothing was happening except that they all looked very silly with a vine wrapped around their wrists.

"Hang on." She frowned at him. "OK. Now everyone stare right at the middle of my hand and don't look away until I tell you."

Jade spoke; soft Elvish words that would make no sense to the others. She blotted out their puzzlement, their breathing, their presence and drew on her inner connection with the great forest around. She allowed her voice to rise and fall in a hypnotic chant; a song that entwined them in the lazy warmth of summer; the blazing colours of autumn; the frost-white chill of winter and the green newness of spring, all intertwined at once. Somehow, the scents of cut hay and ripe berries; new snow and fresh green peas teased their noses. The sounds of birds singing filled their ears then faded away only to swell again in different songs. On Jade's chest, her amulet glowed.

The vine twisted about their limbs began to pulsate and glow a rich, dark green. Her body throbbing with earth-power, Jade pointed a finger and a small, green flame appeared, dancing just above her palm. The vine seemed to slide down their arms, toward the flame. Weirdly, it wasn't getting tighter. In fact, it seemed to be disappearing somewhere. It was absorbed into the flame at the centre of Jade's hand. There was a green, sort of misty look about their hands now.

She finished the spell. The power ebbed from her body and the green mist vanished. The others stared at their hands. The vine was gone. They glanced at Jade and she nodded, drawing her hand back and inspecting it. Phoenix and the others did the same. There was no green mark; no sign of the vine or the mud. Their hands were perfectly clean – apart from the grime acquired while travelling, fighting and not bathing.

"What exactly was that?" Phoenix asked, sounding like he wasn't sure he wanted to know.

She blinked at him. "A Binding spell." She swayed on her feet, feeling lightheaded. Marcus put a hand under her arm to steady her.

"Uh huh." Phoenix paused, still staring at his hand.

"And that is?"

"It just means that we four are bound together until the end of our mutual quest," she explained, sinking back onto the log with a sigh of relief. "It's like an oath but a bit deeper. It means that we are sword-companions; oath-brothers and sisters unbreakably bound by the powers of the four Elements – Earth, Air, Fire and Water. We will do all we can to aid each other. If one of us is in trouble, the others will know it. If one is lost, I should be able to sense what direction to go to find him." She looked at them each in turn as the depth of this bond sank in. "Only treachery or death can break this spell. If it's broken, you'll get a sharp pain in the hand and the vine will reappear around mine."

There was a long silence while the others stared at her and digested the implications of the Binding Spell. Brynn looked at Jade with something akin to hero worship in his big brown eyes. Marcus rubbed his thumb across the palm of his hand and shuddered in superstitious reaction. Phoenix shook himself as though trying to rid himself of the clinging sensations of her magic.

"O...K...then..." He clapped Brynn on the shoulder. "Let's get on with it, shall we? Lead on, oh faithful guide."

*****

In his sleep, thousands of kilometres away, Long Baiyu smiled. The purple-blue shimmering aura of magic around him brightened. Strength pulsed faintly in his cold, curled body.

*****

With a new sense of unity, Phoenix, Jade, Brynn and Marcus walked on in damp silence for three hours in a roughly south-westerly direction. Nothing stirred in the sodden forest and the rain showed no sign of letting up. Phoenix began to consider where they would sleep and how they would find and cook food. He carried the two small pigeons, half-smoked above last night's fire. It would be a meagre supper if that were all they had to eat tonight. His stomach already rumbled audibly.

"Brynn," he called out.

The boy stopped and looked back, brows raised. He had an endearing smear of mud across one cheek and the beginnings of dark circles beneath his bright eyes. Phoenix glanced at Jade and saw she, too, looked tired and distracted. She kept staring around at the trees as though she was looking for something or someone. Marcus's mouth was set in a grim, straight line. They needed to rest and plan.

"How far do we go today?" he asked Brynn.

The boy narrowed his eyes and studied the faint path winding between huge oaks ahead. "Maybe another two hours at most?" He sounded uncertain. "We went by the main road with my brother, so it's hard to know exactly how far away we are."

"But where are we headed? It'd be nice to stay somewhere warm and dry tonight," Phoenix added. "I don't like our luck hunting or finding dry firewood in this weather."

"I'd a mind to reach the next village tonight," Brynn agreed. "We can't stay in a tavern with you two." He jerked a thumb at Jade and Marcus. "But I've a maternal aunt who'd be willing to house us for fair pay."

"She wouldn't betray us to the soldiers?" Marcus asked sharply.

Brynn cast him a scornful glance. "Nay, she'd not. She knows what happened to my family and she'd not turn me over to the invaders for anything. I know my kin."

"I'm sorry," the Roman murmured, flushing

"OK," Phoenix said, "we can make it that far, can't we?" He sent a sidelong glance at Jade.

She nodded but closed her eyes briefly. He got the impression that the magic she'd performed had taken a lot out of her.

He made a quick decision. "First we need to find somewhere dry to rest and eat something. We're all tired and if we keep pushing ourselves someone will injure themselves – or worse, we won't be able to defend ourselves against unexpected enemies."

"What about there?" Marcus put in, pointing a little off to the right of the path.

They all squinted through the drizzle. Jade gasped, her face alight. He was pointing at a massive oak tree about fifty metres away. Its branches were so widespread as to shade the ground twenty metres in each direction. Its trunk was so thick that ten people could stand, arms stretched with fingertips touching, and still not encompass it. A million tiny, new green leaves sparkled on every branch and twig. It was a thing of beauty. There was a narrow, dark breach in one side – only wide enough to admit a man's shoulders.

"Perfect!" Jade breathed. "So that's what I've been hearing. I knew she had to be around here somewhere."

"It's just a big, hollow tree, isn't it?" Brynn asked. "How can you hear a tree?"

She smiled secretively. "Yep, just a big, hollow tree."

"So why don't I trust that smile?" Phoenix stared at her.

She punched him on the arm. "C'mon. Let's go."

"Wait!" Marcus called. They all looked at him. "Did you hear that?" He stood still with one finger raised, turning his head slowly.

The others stopped and listened hard. Nothing. Brynn opened his mouth to make a smart comment when they all heard it – the sound of many, stealthy feet creeping inexpertly through the sodden forest around them.

Jade closed her eyes and turned in a circle. "Romans," she stated. "About fifty of them." She opened her eyes. "I was too busy listening to the tree to hear them before. There are too many for me to put a control spell on and too many to fight." Frowning, she looked around and shivered. "There's something else out there, too. I can't tell what. Something that's…hunting the Romans. It's hungry." Clutching at Phoenix's arm, she stared at him, wide-eyed. "It's getting closer and so are the soldiers. We have to move, now!" She tugged him toward the great tree.

Phoenix hesitated, drawing his weapon. He'd prefer to fight his way out again, than to hide like a coward. He glanced around, seeing flashes of red through the undergrowth on either side of the path. They'd prevailed once; surely they could do it again? Jade yanked again at his arm even as she gave Brynn a push toward the tree.

"What's the point of hiding in a tree?" Phoenix growled. "They'll know we're there and just smoke us out or burn the tree." Jade snorted and he glanced around at the soggy forest.

"OK," Phoenix growled, "then they'll just wait us out. We can't stay in there forever! We should fight."

"Go, Marcus!" Jade insisted. "Now, Brynn. Run!" She turned back to Phoenix and muttered fiercely. "Trust me on this. The Romans are the least of our worries. We do not want to be here when that…thing that's hunting *them* arrives. I promise we will not be trapped inside but you have to run now!" When he still didn't move, she sent him a despairing look, let go and dashed away toward the great tree with long, swift strides. Her hood fell back and her long hair fluttered like a tattered, wet flag behind her.

All three of his companions were now almost at the dark entrance to the tree. Phoenix stood, still undecided. The adrenalin rush of battle surged through his Warrior's body. He wanted to fight them. He was strong. Why should he run?

Phoenix heard a twig crack behind him. Suddenly, the kid in him realised the idea of fighting fifty trained Roman soldiers and one beast of the Dark Woods on his own was pretty insane. There was bravery and then there was sheer stupidity. He wasn't stupid.

He ran.

Behind him, Phoenix heard shouts of anger and frustration as the Romans realised the last of their prey was escaping. The sound of many feet running, branches snapping, leather armour creaking and weapons clanging dogged his footsteps. They gained. He had only about twenty metres to go. He was going to make it!

Four soldiers stepped out onto the path ahead, blocking his escape. They lowered pila and waited with set faces and planted feet for him to impale himself. More appeared to either side so he couldn't leave the path. Phoenix saw and gritted his teeth. Instead of stopping, he increased speed. The soldiers looked slightly anxious. When he was only metres away from the end of their speartips, they looked downright worried.

Inside, Phoenix was worried as well. He thought he could do what he intended but part of him wasn't sure: the thirteen-year-old part. Pushing fear aside, he drew a deep breath and screamed the loudest, most terrifying war cry he could summon. One of the soldiers took an involuntary step back, shocked by the ferocity of this suicidal Breton Warrior. The tips of two javelins lowered slightly.

Phoenix made his move. With a mighty effort, he increased his speed again and bunched his thigh muscles. Then he sprang.

It was an impossible leap – especially since he somersaulted in mid-air and sliced down and back with his sword as he went. The blade connected with the unprotected back of one soldier who then fell heavily against his companions, clutching at their arms. It caused enough confusion that Phoenix was able to complete his manoeuvre unchallenged. In the real world, he would have simply crashed headlong into the Roman soldiers or been skewered by their spears. Fortunately, in this world, it seemed the impossible was sometimes possible, if you believed it.

He landed lightly, allowed his legs to collapse and executed a reasonable Aikido roll. Letting his momentum carry him, he came to his feet and dashed the last few steps to the tree. Shouts and footfalls behind him said he was only just ahead of his pursuers. He stripped the shield from his back as he ran and slid sideways into the narrow gap. It was a tight squeeze into dubious safety.

Inside the tree, he skidded to a stop in pitch-blackness and utter silence. Confused, Phoenix spun to look for the opening. There ought to be light, or at least angry Romans, coming through it. There was nothing.

Fighting rising panic, he blinked a couple of times and rubbed his eyes. Was he blind? The darkness was so absolute it almost felt thick; the silence so complete he could hear only his own harsh breathing and creaking leather. Cautiously, he reached out and turned a slow circle – but touched nothing.

"Hello?" His voice sounded muffled; the blackness a blanket soaking up sound and light. Clearing his throat, he tried again. "Jade? Marcus? Brynn?"

There was no answer.

****

CHAPTER THIRTEEN

Drawing three long, deep breaths to calm himself, Phoenix tried to slow his thundering heart. He had to think. He'd gone into the body of the huge oak tree. Brynn, Marcus and Jade had all done the same. Logically, they should be here.

Where was 'here'? This thick, heavy blackness didn't fit with his idea of what the inside of a tree should look like. There should be dirt, wooden walls; maybe some water dripping; a few bugs; even bats. Not nothing at all.

He jumped up and down a few times. The floor felt soft underfoot but when he reached a hand down, he couldn't actually tell where the ground began. It was a weird sensation. His fingers met resistance, but he couldn't feel anything with his fingertips.

He sheathed his sword and re-hung his shield over his back. Pulling out flint-and-tinder, he attempted to strike a light by touch alone. Even though he could hear the rock and iron clicking together, there weren't any visible sparks. Angry and frightened, Phoenix tucked them away again with jerky movements and wished for an electric torch. He drew a deep breath.

"Brynn! Marcus! Jade! Where the heck is everyone?" His voice sounded thin and stifled.

Something touched his shoulder. He yelped, spinning and half-drawing his sword in quick reaction. A hand grabbed his, forcing it down.

"Wait!" It was Marcus's voice, also strangely quiet. "It's me."

Phoenix was almost sick with relief and glad the Roman boy couldn't see his face. He slid his sword into the scabbard and gripped the other's arm.

"Where are we? Where're Brynn and Jade?"

"Brynn's here with me," Marcus replied, a little louder now.

Phoenix felt a warm breath on his arm. Brynn's small hand found his and held on. Even though it gave him the creeps not to be able to see the others, he didn't pull away. He needed their company right now and it felt like they needed his.

"Jade?"

There was a pause and Phoenix's stomach lurched. Had she been captured? Then Brynn's voice replied shakily from somewhere down by his elbow.

"She's…carrying us."

Again, Phoenix was glad they couldn't see him. He just knew there was a totally stupid, blank look on his face. Brynn must have sensed his confusion, for he continued.

"We didn't have time to warn you. We're inside the Hyllion Bagia."

Phoenix choked back shock. His knees sagged little. "How? Why? And most importantly: how do we get out?"

Brynn renewed his grip on Phoenix's hand. "It was the best idea we could come up with," he said meekly. "I said you wouldn't like it but Jade insisted. We were inside the oak tree, watching the Romans corner you." The boy squeezed Phoenix's hand. "Brilliant jump, by the way."

Phoenix couldn't help but grin, even though the boy couldn't see. He cleared his throat and frowned. "So how is being in the bag supposed to help us? If she gets caught by the Romans we'll be stuck here forever." Anger, pushed on by fear, built in his guts. This was what he got for trusting anyone but himself. If there was no-one on the outside to call their names, they might never escape this magic prison!

"No, no!" Brynn tugged on his arm. "She won't get caught. The Romans won't find her."

Phoenix snorted. "Right. Like there are so many places she can hide inside a tree. She'll be caught and imprisoned and we'll never get out of here. Don't get me wrong," he added. "I like you guys, but I don't fancy the idea of being trapped in a magic bag for the rest of my life with you." With a frustrated grunt he shook himself free of Brynn's clutch.

Marcus grabbed his elbow again, his fingers tightening and finding sensitive pressure points until Phoenix yelped in surprise.

"If you'll give us a chance, we can explain," he said quietly.

Phoenix subsided, muttering, "Fine. Explain then." He had been behaving like a fool, but it was really annoying to have Marcus point it out.

Brynn drew a deep, shaky breath. "Jade said the oak tree belongs to the Dryads – I think she meant the tree Twlwyth Teg, the Faery folk," he explained as Phoenix drew breath to ask what the heck a Dryad was.

"Yes," Marcus struck in, "Dryad is the Greek word for the tree folk."

Brynn hurried on. "She knew that she could gain access to the Faery-realm through the tree, but we wouldn't be allowed and neither would the Romans. So…."

"So, she stuck us in a magic bag and here we are," Phoenix finished, "waiting to find out if she really did escape into some other land or not. Great." He sighed and reached out in the pitch black to find Brynn's thin shoulder. Squeezing it, he tried to let the kid know there were no hard feelings. He wasn't very good at apologising.

"So, what do we do now?" he asked the darkness.

"We wait." Marcus's calm reply came after a short pause.

Phoenix groaned. "Somehow I knew you were going to say that."

****

Jade stuffed the Bagia into her pack and glanced over her shoulder. The entrance to the oak shelter darkened with the approach of angry soldiers. Placing a hand on the wood either side of the split, she spoke to the great tree in Elvish. With a deep, creaking groan, the tree shuddered in response.

Yells of surprise sounded outside as the opening began to creak closed. Jade kept her hands on the walls, willing the tree to heal itself faster; to close the entrance enough so the soldiers couldn't get in.

A spear jabbed through the hole. Jade gasped and just managed to swivel her body aside. It missed her stomach by millimetres. The leering face of a Roman soldier appeared in the narrowing gap. She backed away. The opening was too narrow to admit a man now, but he could still see her.

He laughed coarsely. "That's ok, girlie. You stay right there. We're getting axes and we'll have you out soon enough."

Frightened and angry, Jade stepped forward and poked two long fingers through, into the man's squinting eyes. He screamed and fell back into the arms of his companions. The crack closed a few more inches. Desperately, she looked around. She couldn't allow the tree to be injured. The Dryads would never forgive her if she let the Romans hack at it with axes.

Leaning her forehead against the wood, she asked the great life another question and gave it certain instructions. There was a suggestion of slow thought and agreement, followed by a brief, confusing sense of one-ness; a moment when Jade felt like she was part of the tree. She completely understood the problems of too little sun and too much rain; the annoyance of small burrowing insects and the joy of sheltering living things; the sorrow of watching their warm, brief lives pass; the sleep of winter and the rebirth of spring. Her own problems seemed insignificant.

Smiling, Jade lifted her head and looked about. A small door had appeared in the timber next to her.

A deep, snarling roar reverberated through the Dark

Woods, startling her in the act of reaching for the doorhandle. She peered out then flinched back at the sight of a full-grown ogre emerging from the forest behind the Romans. Standing well over four metres, its gnarled, wood-coloured skin looked as tough as old oak. Each of four muscular arms ended in six-fingered hands tipped in razor-sharp claws. A small head sat on broad shoulders. Its eight beady, black eyes were placed strategically so it could see in all directions. Most frightening of all was the mouth full of jagged sabre-teeth designed to slice through skin and bone without effort.

Jade shrank into the darkness as the Romans formed up ranks. They didn't seem very happy when their officers ordered an attack. A pilum and dozens of arrows bounced off its thick skin, serving only to enrage it. The ogre casually picked up the closest soldier and shook him until things cracked and he stopped yelling.

Jade's stomach heaved.

The monster picked up a second soldier, using him as a club to bowl over a half-dozen of his companions.

The Romans broke rank at last, ignoring their officers in favour of running for their lives. The ogre stayed, sitting down amongst the dead. He chortled and growled, surrounded by a pathetic pile of scarlet and leather, flesh and bone. He picked up an arm and sniffed it.

Jade closed her eyes to the carnage, grateful that she had an escape route that didn't involve going past that beast. Even so, she would have nightmares for days. She patted the wood thankfully then slipped through the portal. It closed behind her and disappeared.

Jade entered the Dryad realm with fear in her heart. Yes, the great oak had called to her, even accepted and helped her. The Dryads would already be aware of that. Surely, they would be hospitable to a half-elf if their trees were. She wasn't certain of her reception, though. Her character's human mother had kept her away from the great forest and its inhabitants. She didn't even know who her Elvish father was. She was just hoping and praying that the tree-faery folk would accept her as kin – or at least let her pass through unharmed. If they didn't...

It was frightening to feel so alone. The others' lives were, literally, in her hands. If she failed they would all die.

Swallowing her fears down as best she could, Jade drew a shaky breath. Clenching her hands around her staff, she trod through a dimly-lit tunnel. The walls were hard to see. They seemed to be wooden, but she couldn't be sure. Each time she looked directly at them, they appeared shift and move until her eyes almost crossed in an effort to focus. Even eerier was the feeling that she travelled great distances with every small step. The ground slid beneath her feet. She truly was in the Anoeth – the Timeless Land. Jade shook her head and tried hard to ignore the weirdness.

Gradually, the tunnel brightened and the walls and floor assumed the more comfortable appearance of packed earth. Ahead, a narrow wooden door appeared. Even its handle and hinges were wood. She stopped at the doorway and took a deep breath. Nervousness fluttered in her stomach.

Lifting the latch-handle, she eased the door open and peered around it. Beyond lay a large, lofty, windowless room decorated in soft autumn shades and lit by a gentle, golden glow from some unknown source. The walls were of living wood. This room was, somehow, inside the great oak tree.

Throwing her shoulders back, Jade stepped in and closed the door gently behind.

"So..." A soft, yet layered, voice by her side made her jump and gasp. "My tree tells me you claim sanctuary in our land, young one? You have brought our enemy to our doorstep; to my beloved tree. I had to call a Guardian to dispose of them. By what right do you now ask for our help?"

Jade looked at the tall, extraordinary woman beside her and instinctively did the right thing: she dropped to one knee and bowed her head in utmost respect. This was, without a doubt, the grande dame of the tree-folk. She had to be the dryad who guarded the giant oak.

"My Lady," she choked, "I..I meant no disrespect. I am sorry if I've placed your tree in danger. I heard her in my mind and didn't know where else to go in this forest."

The dryad cut her off but not unkindly. "I understand, girl, but state your case quickly. I felt your passage through my Forest. The only reason you still live is that you spared the Strangler when you could have killed it. For this you have been left alone by the Dark Folk and admitted to my presence. Speak or I shall have you returned to the Romans who await without – or what's left of them."

When Jade could not find her voice, the Dryad spoke again, a little less harshly.

"I am Aurfanon. What may I call you?" Her name translated to Gold Queen.

Jade risked another quick look at this fascinating lady.

At first glimpse, she had seemed young and stunning with golden skin, amber eyes and rippling hair the rich red of autumn leaves. Now, as Jade looked again, she could see physical signs of age – a few strands of grey in that luxurious hair; a few crows' feet wrinkles around the almond-shaped eyes. The dryad stood straight and firm with a reassuring aura of strength and wisdom, but she was old beyond human understanding. Even though she wore only a simple, long dress of white linen and a wreath of golden oak leaves in her hair, the dryad carried herself like the queen she undoubtedly was.

Jade managed to get her brain engaged and replied, giving her character name rather than her own.

"My Lady, I am called Jade gan Eleri of the Cyfriniol forest. I seek only safe passage across Anoeth to escape from Roman soldiers who seek to capture and torture me."

The lady stiffened. She was silent a moment and Jade wondered if she'd said something wrong.

"Rise, child," the dryad said after a moment, "and sit with me awhile."

Confused and relieved, Jade stood and followed her hostess to a nearby pile of cushions. Easing her backpack onto the floor, she crossed her legs beneath the low table standing between her and the dryad queen.

The door opened and another, younger dryad entered, bearing a tray. She glanced at Jade but didn't speak. Aurfanon waved her out once the tray rested on the table. Jade eyed the array of enticing foods and tried not to drool. The queen did not invite her to eat, so she resolutely turned her eyes away.

Aurfanon watched her with open curiosity.

"You said your name was Jade gan Eleri? Jade, daughter of Eleri?" she asked. Jade nodded. "Is your mother Eleri, Spellweaver of the great Cyfriniol forest? Eleri daughter of Brychan, the hunter?"

Jade nodded again, blinking in shock as she searched her dual memories and confirmed to herself the names of her mother and maternal grandfather. How could the queen possibly know that? Yes, she was a half-elf but she never expected to be even recognised by the Faery, let alone have her human ancestry known to a dryad queen.

Aurfanon smiled faintly and waved a hand at the loaded plates before them.

"Eat, child." She reached out and patted Jade's hand. "Then you must tell me of your troubles and I will see what I can do to help. I knew your mother a little."

****

Time passed. Or, at least, Phoenix assumed it passed. It was hard to tell when he was stuck in a bag.

It took him a while to come to terms with the need to simply sit and wait for Jade to get them out. Having a Warrior body and Warrior brain, added to his own natural impulse to be moving and doing, meant he wanted action. He'd had enough of waiting and hoping in the real world. With nowhere to go in the Bag, he paced and fretted. Finally, frustrated, he practiced aikido kata in an attempt to get his warrior body to do what he wanted it to. It sort of worked but he still felt stupidly unco-ordinated and got more frustrated as his body didn't respond as easily to the moves as in the real world. At last, even Brynn's cheerful patience wore out and the boy snapped at him to sit down.

After that, they sat on the unseen, unfelt floor and shared out the remains of what edible food they had. Brynn produced some sort of whistle and piped lilting, sweet tunes until he ran out of songs and had to stop for breath. Afterward, they talked in snatches for a while; but the conversation eventually petered out, stifled by the darkness. Nothing changed. It was still suffocatingly dark and mind-numbingly boring.

Marcus fell asleep with the amazing ability of a seasoned soldier to rest when and where he can. His deep, even breaths were barely audible. Even Brynn gave up his usual pert chatter in the face of the Hyllion Bagia's strange muffling. He leaned against Phoenix's shoulder and occasionally sighed.

In due course, Phoenix must have fallen asleep as well, for the next thing he knew, Marcus was shaking him.

"Wake up."

"Wha…?" He blinked in the darkness and rubbed gritty eyes, but it was still dark. "What's going on? Why'd you wake me up?"

"Something's happening." Marcus's hand still gripped Phoenix's shoulder. "Wake Brynn."

Phoenix shook the younger boy and all three stared into the thick darkness.

"So?" Phoenix asked. "What's happening? I don't see anything."

"I'm sure I heard Jade's voice," Marcus assured him.

Phoenix sighed. "You were probably dreaming."

"No," the other replied, unperturbed, "I'm certain I heard her; and there was a flash of light for a moment, like she'd opened the bag."

"Well, if she did that," Phoenix pointed out, "why didn't she say our names and get us out?"

"I don't know," Marcus had a hint of impatience in his normally-calm voice, "but she might at any moment and I thought you'd like to be awake for it, rather than half-asleep."

Phoenix grunted, wondering if the eternal darkness and freakiness of this place was finally getting to the calmest member of their little band. It was nice to know something could ruffle Marcus's cool feathers.

"There!" Brynn's high-pitched shout jolted Phoenix out of his musings.

A flash of light overhead made him look up. Surely this was Jade hauling them out of oblivion.

What he saw silhouetted against the light wasn't Jade's hand. Instead, it was a puzzlingly large, curved object that seemed to be both falling towards them and yet falling away from them at the same time. It appeared to be getting closer but in a strange twist of logic-defying physics, it also shrank as it got nearer.

The three boys stood, dumbstruck, staring up at the object for several moments before the light vanished and took with it their ability to see anything at all.

"Ummmm…" Brynn began, "I wonder where that thing will fa—" Thunk!

"OW!" Phoenix clapped his hands to his head and howled in pain. "Ow! Bloody Ow ow ow ow!" He doubled over, grasping his head tightly as if pressure would somehow reduce the agony. Using more swear words than he even knew he knew, he stamped on the non-ground until even swearing and stamping wasn't helping any more.

"You alright?" Brynn's concern didn't help, nor did

Marcus's soft snort of amusement.

"Whatever that was," Phoenix replied crossly, "it hurt! Man!" He fingered his scalp. "I've got a lump the size of a chicken egg on my head." He glared up at where the light had been and shook his fist before realising the gesture was wasted because no-one could see him. "What the heck was Jade thinking, tossing something in with us like that? She could have killed me! What was it, anyway?"

"I don't know," Brynn replied, too cheerfully. "I can't find it now. I think it's part of the bag's magic. You called our names when you came in, so we found you. Since we don't know what Jade threw in, we can't name it and so we can't find it."

Phoenix rubbed his scalp gently. "So if I said, 'pilum', one would—"

"Don't!" Marcus cried, too late.

"Ow! Bloody ow again!" Phoenix yelled.

A Roman spear had whacked him on the arm. Ruefully, he rubbed his elbow and had to laugh.

"That was pretty stupid. At least it wasn't the pointy end."

Brynn giggled.

"Well..." Marcus tactfully didn't complete the sentence.

"Still," Phoenix said at last, "I guess I'm just lucky she didn't toss something sharper in with us." Marcus and Brynn chuckled.

There was a companionable silence for a few moments then Brynn spoke again.

"Did you hear that?"

"What?" Marcus and Phoenix asked together.

"I thought I heard someone call my name," Brynn replied doubtfully. There was a few seconds of silence as they all strained to hear. "Oh well." The boy laughed nervously. "Just wishful think—"

There was a brief flash of blinding light. Before

Phoenix could react, the comforting pressure of Brynn's thin leg against his own was gone. Phoenix leapt up with a shout of alarm.

"Wait!" Marcus's yell and firm hand brought him up short. "The only person who could have got Brynn out of here was Jade." His words were annoyingly reasonable. "She'll call us next, so just be patient."

Phoenix growled. Once again, he'd reacted first and thought later. It was so frustrating to have the Roman boy showing him up by being so darned chill all the time. Phoenix scraped his fingers roughly through his hair. He had to get a handle on himself. Surely, he hadn't always been like this? It must be this stupid digital warrior's fault.

Back at home he'd been really good at thinking before he acted – or at least, he'd learned to be more that way after his mother remarried. Come to think of it, he frowned in the darkness, his real father used to tease him about being too reactive; too quick to get angry. He smiled, remembering many bruises, skinned knees and hands from his youthful schoolyard fights and daring adventures. He'd soon learned to curb his hazardous activities with Jacob watching his every move. Being grounded and threatened was good incentive to restrain himself. OK, so maybe being here in 80AD was just giving him an excuse to go back to his old, stupid ways. Maybe that wasn't such a good thing after all.

"Marcus, do you think—"

There was another bright flash of light and the last Phoenix saw of Marcus was the boy's startled, upturned face.

Then it was dark. He was alone. Again.

"Man," he muttered, fingering his still-sore head, "I'm really getting sick of this."

****

CHAPTER FOURTEEN

Phoenix stumbled, blinking in the clear morning sunlight. Marcus steadied him as Jade tucked the magic bag into her pack.

Boy, she was tired. The trip from the Faery realm took longer than expected. Lead by one of the younger dryads, she'd covered over two days walk in little over half a night. Sometime after midnight the dryad disappeared, and Jade assumed she was on her own again.

After using minor magic to find a suitable, dry hollow log, she managed to sleep restlessly for a couple of hours before waking at dawn. Any hope of getting more rest before pulling the others out of the bag vanished after a quick peek at a nearby village. The hamlet was quite large and several people were already heading into the woods to hunt or forage. If she slept any longer unguarded, someone was certain to find her.

Reluctantly, Jade retreated further into the woods. Feeling rather like a Las Vegas illusionist, she hauled her companions out of the bag one at a time. Brynn popped out all chirpy and full of how interesting it had been to be stuck in the bag. She needed his help to pull Marcus out next. The Roman boy thanked them politely before closely inspecting Jade's. He pursed his lips but said only that she looked tired. Jade was grateful he hadn't scolded her. It took all three of them to heave Phoenix out.

He looked tired as well but more than a little pleased to be out in the world again. Heaving a sigh of relief, he sucked in a deep breath of cool forest air and spread his arms wide.

"Man, am I glad to be out of there. I'm starving and thirsty and I really have to take a leak." He shook his empty water bottle. Jade pointed silently at a nearby stream cascading over dark rocks.

While the others refreshed themselves in various ways, Jade kept watch, wondering if she'd make through the day without falling asleep on her feet. The thought of another day of hard walking made her want to just sit down and refuse to move. She was beyond tired.

It was all just too much to process; too much to cope with. She'd hardly slept for days; fought peasants and Romans, talked to trees and Dryads; Healed wounds and saved lives. Wasn't that enough? Didn't she deserve a break? Maybe if she just put her head down on this log for a few minutes…

"Jade, wake up." It was Phoenix's voice; his hand on her shoulder. "We can't stay here. We've got to get to Stonehenge before the Romans, remember? C'mon, get up."

Jade shoved his hand off, rolling away so he wouldn't see the tears of exhaustion in her eyes. "Go away, Phoenix. Leave me alone. I'm tired. I can't do this anymore. I don't care."

"Come on," he scoffed. "You've just had a cruisey night with the Dryads when we've been stuck in a bag. How bad could it have been?"

She jolted upright, glaring at him. "Cruisey? I spent most the night walking. I've taken two days off our trip while you've been sleeping. You're welcome, by the way." Turning her face away, she clenched her fists, trying to keep back the salt tears that threatened to drown her eyes. She wouldn't go all girly now. Why didn't anyone ever just say 'thanks, great job'? Why wasn't anything she did ever good enough?

There was a long, awkward silence then Brynn cleared his throat.

"There's a village just over the rise. If I can recognise it, I should be able to tell where we are and how far we still have to go. It might even be a place we can. Do you think you can make it that far, Jade?"

Jade sniffed and scrubbed her sleeve across her face. She stood up, leaning on her staff as the world spun a little. Marcus's arm appeared and she borrowed his strength gratefully.

"I'll be ok. I'm just tired, that's all. I'll make it. We don't really have a choice. Let's go." She followed Brynn, not looking at Phoenix as she passed him. She felt a bit silly for lashing out at him. It wasn't his fault she had agreed to push on through the night. How was he supposed to know she hadn't been given the royal VIP treatment?

Aurfanon had been wonderful but had made it clear that they had a very limited time left to succeed in their first Quest. She had confirmed what the old lady in their limbo vision said: they had to get the Jewel from the Keepers before the Romans and before the Spring Equinox. She'd even revealed that the Keepers were, indeed, the Druids and that the Equinox was only two days away. If they failed to get the Jewel and keep it from the Romans, their Quest would be over. Zhudai would win. Their chance to finish and get home would be gone. In fact, the home they knew would be gone if Zhudai took control of this world. Jade still didn't really understand how that worked but it seemed she had to take it on faith.

Time was running out and with it Jade's confidence. They'd never make in time and she'd be stuck here – her own life lost or destroyed.

Catching her breath on a sob, Jade scrubbed at her face.

"Hey!" Phoenix's voice from behind drew Jade's attention.

She slowed to let him catch up, glad of the distraction from her depression but wary after his previous ungrateful attitude. She really shouldn't have taken her fears out on him, though.

"I'm sorry." "Sorry." They both spoke at once.

Jade caught his eye and joined in with his rueful laughter.

"I shouldn't have snapped at you," she sighed. "It's been a tough couple of days. An ogre came and…ate…some of the Romans while I was in the tree." She shuddered at the gruesome memory.

"Wow! Cool…and…er…gross, I guess." Phoenix paused, obviously not sure what to say to that. "I should have seen how tired you are." He gave her an apologetic grimace. "I guess, when I'm ready to get moving, I sort of expect everyone else should be, too. My mother's always telling me to stop and think before I open my mouth but I suck at it."

She cast him a quick smile. "And my dad always says, 'it takes two to argue'."

He grinned. "My dad said the same thing when I got into fights at school. Well," he amended, "what he actually said was, 'he who strikes first admits he has run out of ideas', but it kind of meant the same thing…probably."

Jade laughed, her ill humour almost gone. She resolutely pushed aside her lingering fears and raised her head to look forward again.

They walked on in silence for awhile. Marcus caught them up. Jade smiled at him. Phoenix sighed and scrubbed stiff fingers through greasy hair. He winced.

Jade caught his look. "You ok?"

He nodded. "Just a bump on the head from whatever you threw in the bag with us last night. What was it, anyway?"

She stared at him, confused then remembered. "Oh, right. That was a gift from Aurfanon."

The two warriors looked at her.

"A horn," she added, when Phoenix gestured for her to continue. "I'm supposed to blow it if we get into real trouble and help will come."

"Sweet!" Phoenix's blue eyes lit with eager excitement. "That's more like it. A really useful magic item. About time, too".

Jade glanced at Marcus and saw that he, too looked impressed, if a bit uneasy.

"Yeah," she agreed, "but we can only use it three times and only if we're in truly dire peril and..." She raised a warning finger. "The help we get might not always be what we expect."

Phoenix looked irritated by the limitations. "What does that mean?"

"No idea." Jade shrugged, a yawn distorting her words. "I'm just repeating what Aurfanon said. Three times; dire emergency; unpredictable outcome."

"Still..." Phoenix slapped a hand on her shoulder. "It's an extra trick up our sleeves we didn't have before. Better than nothing."

She shrugged again, her whole body drooping with exhaustion.

"Listen," he frowned at her. "Maybe Brynn's right - we can rest up in this village. Give you a chance to get your energy levels up again before we tackle the final part of this level."

"Thanks, Phoenix," she sighed, "but we really don't have time."

"What do you mean? Surely if you've gained us so much ground we're well ahead of the Romans now?"

She shook her head, repeating what the Dryad queen had told her about the Equinox and the Druids being the Keepers of the Jewel.

Phoenix groaned, rubbing a dirty hand across his forehead. "Well, at least we know who has it. Now we just have to find them before this Equinox thing. Only two days? That's it? Man, we don't even know where we are yet. What's so important about the Spring Equinox, anyway? What is an Equinox?"

*****

Brynn's soft call cut short whatever explanation Jade had been about to embark on - which was good, as Phoenix regretted his impulsive question the second it left his lips. He didn't actually care what an Equinox was, as long as it wasn't going to attack them. Brynn was crouched behind a tree, waving frantically at them to take cover. Phoenix hurried to his side and peered around the bole of the tree. Below, cleared ground sloped away from the forest, down toward a fortified village. They had approached the town from the south-west through the last stands of trees.

Brynn pointed and whispered. "We've been lucky. The dryads brought us over the Plowonida, through the worst of the Dywyllwch Brennau and out the other side. That's the river Kennet, just north and the village is Cunetio. It used to be just farmland but now it's Roman. See?"

Surrounding the small settlement was a two metre high defensive wall of earth with a deep ditch on its outside. Marcus informed them there would be a similar ditch directly inside the earth wall. Peaked, red-tiled roofs of at least twenty stone and wood buildings were visible neatly lined up inside the fortified area.

Two major roads bisected the town, one leading east-west and one north-west to south-east. Brynn pointed to the latter. "That's the road we'll need to follow to get to the Great Stone Circle. We follow it for about three hours then turn south-west, cross a small river and we're there." The boy glanced up at Phoenix. "If we leave now, we could just about make it by nightfall even if we stick to the fields."

Phoenix looked longingly at the town, thinking of beds, decent food and shelter. He heard dogs and children running about with barks and shrieks of laughter. A group of four women walked into the village carrying buckets made of animal hide. Water slopped on the ground as the women chatted and laughed. A farmer led a plow-beast out to a nearby field. The scene looked harmless: domestic and peaceful. Surely, they could risk one night for the sake of a decent sleep and full stomachs?

He looked at his companions, intending to announce that they should spend the night in Cunetio. Jade's face was drawn and resigned; Brynn eyed the town with yearning and fear; Marcus's handsome face was hard, his return gaze unblinking. Staring at their expressions, Phoenix hesitated. The decision wasn't his alone. If he were captured, the worst he could expect was to be forcibly drafted into the Roman army. Jade and Marcus would suffer far worse fates. Brynn would probably be made into a slave or servant, at best. As much as Phoenix wanted to, he had no right to make this decision for them. Reluctantly, he pushed aside his own desire.

"What do you guys think we should do? Should we stay here and get some rest? Or should we push on and try to get closer to Carega Amgarn?"

There was approval in Marcus's dark eyes. Jade and Brynn exchanged looks before replying together.

"We push on."

Marcus nodded his agreement.

Phoenix suppressed a sharp twinge of regret. "Fair enough but we need to find somewhere warm, comfortable and safe to sleep, agreed?"

"Agreed," the others chorused wholeheartedly.

So, they shouldered their burdens once more and gave Cunetio and its promise of comfort a wide berth. As they slipped away, Jade reached out for Phoenix's hand and gave it a quick squeeze. Phoenix gripped her slim fingers in return, feeling more at peace with himself than he had for many months. Perhaps his father had been onto something about this 'do the right thing' business.

Two nights before, Marcus had assumed him to be the leader of this expedition. At the time, Phoenix had almost laughed. He'd never been the leader of anything – not even his football team. It had been an attractive idea, though.

Leader. He'd spent quite a while in the Bag, thinking about it. After all, leaders got to tell people what to do and they had to do it. They had control; they had power. That was what he'd wanted when he started this game: control over his own life; the power to make his own decisions.

Now he had to rethink the whole thing. Maybe being a leader wasn't just ordering and being obeyed. Maybe it was more…

Phoenix frowned, unable to follow the thought through to completion. He didn't know what it was; only that it wasn't just being a bossy control freak. Leadership was something entirely different. But what?

Unable to come to a conclusion, he sighed and shelved the idea for later thought. Right now he just had to make sure they all made it to Stonehenge before the Romans and before the Spring Equinox thingy.

In spite of the lack of covering forests in this part of the country, the travellers made good time. They stayed away from the road, moving along edges of fields and keeping a close eye out for Roman Centuria. Whenever those distinctive scarlet and leather uniforms appeared, the four immediately sought cover.

Since it was spring, the field crops weren't yet high enough to hide in but there were plenty of hedges, stone walls, small shepherd's huts and groves of trees. Once, however, the party was obliged to throw themselves flat amongst the ploughed furrows and stay perfectly still as a Roman runner-messenger sped past in the distance.

When the sound of running feet disappeared, Jade raised her head and stared down the road. "I wonder why he was in such a hurry."

"What do you mean?" Phoenix wasn't particularly worried by a non-threatening runner.

Jade frowned. "I might just be paranoid but that's the third messenger we've seen on the road this morning. I'm just worried that Feng Zhudai might be on our trail."

Phoenix looked at her in astonishment. "But how could he?" He glanced around the open fields, hands spread. "You cut two days off our trip. How could the Cohort looking for Marcus possibly catch up to us – or even know where we're going in the first place?"

She grimaced. "I don't know. I just know there's something wrong. I feel...uneasy."

He chuckled. "That's an understatement. Of course there's something wrong. This whole place is wrong on several levels." He grinned. "If you'll forgive the pun."

Jade didn't respond in kind. She just shook her head. "Don't forget that Zhudai is some sort of arch-wizard. If we do have to win through all five lev...quests, - and we succeed by some fluke - then he's in big trouble." She gripped Phoenix's arm and dropped her voice to a whisper. "Is it possible he could know what our task is for each level of the game and try and stop us?"

Phoenix stared at her for a moment, deciding she looked so worried he should at least consider her words. Then he shook his head firmly.

"No, that's just paranoid. There's hundreds of players, remember? Zhudai couldn't possibly be in all places trying to thwart all of them at once."

"Yes," she said slowly, "but they're not here yet and we are. We're here for a reason, remember? We're the only ones with..." she tapped her chest and raised an eyebrow significantly, reminding him of their amulets.

"As far as we know," he returned. "Let's get moving and stop trying to second-guess ourselves. We have a Jewel thing to steal, remember?" He gestured for Brynn to keep moving and they all fell into line again.

"Oh, I remember." Jade nodded vigorously. "And do you remember that we still have no idea how we're going to steal it or even what it looks like?"

"I know, I know." He flicked a hand at her, irritated by her persistence. They'd work it out as they went.

Jade wouldn't let it go. "Phoenix," she insisted, grabbing his arm and pulling him up short, "we have to have a plan. We can't just run in waving swords around like idiots and expect the Jewel to fall into our laps. At least we know the Keepers are the Druids but how are we going to get the Jewel from the Druids?"

"I could always just ask Dewydd to get it for us," Brynn's clear voice piped up.

****

CHAPTER FIFTEEN

Jade and Phoenix stopped in their tracks, staring down at the boy.

"Who," Phoenix sounded like he was holding irritated impatience in check by sheer willpower, "is Dewydd?"

Brynn gave them a look of wide-eyed innocence. "My brother, of course – the one my Da and I brought here to become a Druid. Remember?"

Jade covered her eyes with her hand and groaned. How could they have forgotten that? Phoenix threw his head back and sighed. Marcus raised surprised brows.

"I'd completely forgotten about your brother." Phoenix slapped a hand to his forehead.

"I never knew about him," Marcus said.

Jade laughed, the thought of an easy solution lifting her spirits.

Phoenix crouched in the turned earth, staring hard at Brynn. "Do you think Dewydd would be willing to help us?"

"Won't know until I ask, will I?" The boy grinned lopsidedly. "He'll be glad to see me, I know that."

"Well, as plans go, it's not foolproof." Phoenix scraped his fingers through his hair and stood up. "But I guess it's worth a shot. It'd certainly be the easiest way to complete our quest." He sent a quick look at Marcus and Jade, and gave them a twisted smile. "But it would be a bit anticlimactic."

"I could gladly skip a few battles and chases for a little success and boredom," Jade said fervently.

"Really?" Phoenix returned in mock surprise. "You'd skip a good bloodthirsty skirmish with the Romans, just to get to the next quest?"

Jade pretended to consider his question in all seriousness. "Get home, you mean? Hmmmm. Let me think....Yes, yes, I would. Give me a nice calm and peaceful trade with Brynn's brother any day."

"Well..." Phoenix clapped Brynn and Jade on the back and gave them a little shove in the right direction. "Let's hope that's what you get, but I'll be stunned if it is."

Jade wrinkled her nose at him, annoyed he had to burst her bubble of hope.

With lighter hearts, they made good time for the rest of the morning. By noon, though, Jade was totally wrecked and called a halt. She had reached the end of her energy reserves. Marcus found an abandoned wattle-and-daub hut and they all crowded inside. Phoenix pulled the very unappetising remains of half-smoked bird from his pack. Brynn made a disgusted face. None of them relished the idea of eating it.

Jade, with a smug smile, told Phoenix to throw it away and reached into the Hyllion Bagia. Brynn groaned in appreciation at the sight of dryad-cooked foods spread out on a cloth on before them. There were fruits of every description, nuts, berries and cooked tubers; herb flatbreads; pies and egg-dishes to die for; slow-roasted pork and lamb legs; waterskins containing sweet water, light wines and juices. In humble silence, the four ate until their stomachs bulged. Reverently, they toasted the Faery folk's kindness and culinary skills. Afterward, not surprisingly, they all fell asleep.

Jade dreamt she was washing her face. The water was smelly and sticky and the washcloth felt squishy on her cheek. For some reason, she lay on a very dirty bathroom floor. What the...?

She sat bolt upright – and stifled a shriek as she almost butted heads with a too-friendly, half-grown sheep. It bleated at her before trotting away. In disgust, Jade scrubbed her face with a sleeve. Sheep spit. Eww.

She gasped staring around at her motionless companions in horror. If a sheep had got in here unnoticed, what else had? For a second she thought her friends were dead but a loud snore from Brynn reassured her. A quick glance outside showed no soldiers or farmers nearby – just more stupid sheep. She sighed in relief. They had been incredibly lucky.

With the toe of her boot, she nudged the others awake. Marcus woke instantly, knife in hand. Brynn muttered and batted at her foot before rolling over. She pushed him harder until the boy finally sat up and rubbed his eyes, yawning.

Phoenix heaved himself up, groaning. "Man, what time is it? I feel like a truck hit me."

"What's a truck?" Brynn asked sleepily.

"It's almost dusk." Jade ignored the question. She frowned at the others. "We've all been asleep for several hours."

Phoenix yawned and shrugged. Marcus pursed his lips.

Jade wrapped her arms around herself, shivering. "Luckily, no-one found us except a sheep but we can't let it happen again."

Brynn smothered a giggle and said something she couldn't quite hear about being savaged by fierce sheep.

Jade chose to ignore this wisecrack too. "What do we do? It's almost too dark to go on. Do we stay here? There's more food in the bag if you're hungry."

"But we've only got about an hour more to walk," Brynn urged, "and I'm still stuffed." He rubbed his belly and belched.

"We can't go anywhere in the dark." Phoenix sided with Jade. "Torches are too risky and Jade shouldn't be expected to lead us half-blind idiots around all night. Besides," he added with a glance at Jade's face, "I think we could use some more rest before we attempt to steal the Jewel."

"But if we go now, we can meet the druids tonight and have the Jewel before tomorrow night!" Brynn insisted.

"Why is tonight so important?" Jade frowned at the boy.

"Because tomorrow night will be the night before Spring Equinox." The boy seemed surprised that they had no idea what he was talking about. "Spring Equinox is one of the big occasions for the Druids. It's one of the few times each year when you're absolutely certain to find them at Carega Amgarn. At other times, they're really hard to find." The boy shook his head sadly and cast a half-annoyed, half-apologetic look at Marcus. "The Romans have been trying to wipe out the Druids all over Britain. Two years ago they destroyed the Druid temple at Mona. Most of the time they're in hiding, like the Faery."

The others digested this information in silence for a few moments.

"So why don't we just go tomorrow night to speak to Dewydd?" Jade asked the question they were all thinking.

Brynn stared at them in astonishment, clearly unable to fathom their stupidity. "Because that will be too late. At dawn the next day, they hold the Spring Equinox ceremony – y'know, when the Druids give sacrifices and gifts to the Earth Goddess who makes all the plants grow and the animals thrive." He waved his skinny arms around to indicate the natural world. "They choose the gifts tonight."

"And let me guess," Jade drew the obvious conclusion, "the Jewel of Asgard is destined to be one of those sacrificial gifts to the Earth Goddess."

Brynn blinked at her and nodded. "Of course. That's how I knew he had it. Dewydd told me he had charge of it when he visited us oohhhh, just a few weeks before my parents..." His animated little face fell and Marcus laid a hand on his shoulder. He shrugged it off. "I just didn't know which Stone Circle he'd be at until I met you two. They do the ceremony at a different Circle each year."

"You could have told us earlier, dude. *We* didn't know he had it." Phoenix closed his eyes and pinched the bridge of his nose between two fingers. "So, tell me again how Dewydd is just going to give the Jewel to us?"

"Oh, well," Brynn said sheepishly, "I kinda expected that we could trade something equally valuable – maybe the Hyllion Bagia, or all the stuff in it."

Marcus, Phoenix and Jade all gazed at Brynn in wonder.

"You'd be prepared to give away all that Roman money and the bag to help us complete our quest?" Jade voiced her amazement.

Brynn's mouth firmed. "If it got us closer to killing Feng Zhudai, I'd do just about anything."

The three older companions exchanged looks and nodded in silent agreement. Brynn's determination was infectious. Sleep suddenly didn't seem quite as urgent as the need to keep moving. Without further discussion, they gathered their gear, stole from the hut and headed southwest across the fields.

The sun set in spectacular fashion behind distant hills. For a while they moved more slowly through the gathering dusk; picking their way carefully over furrowed ground. The moon had not yet risen. Before long, it was too dark for the humans to see. Jade took over, leading them through the gathering gloom until they stubbed their toes once too often and she was forced to call a halt.

"Hang on," she rummaged in her herb-bag, "I think I've worked out a spell for this. Everyone hold out a hand." They did as instructed and she placed a small, soft object in each outstretched hand.

"Feels like...moss," Brynn said, sounding surprised.

"It is. Just a moment." Jade muttered a few Elven words and the little bundles of moss began to glow with a soft, greenish light. "If you shield them with your other hand," she instructed, "you should be able to see the ground in front of your feet at least."

"Won't the lights be seen by Romans or farmers?" Marcus queried.

"We don't have much choice. Hopefully they'll just think they're will-o-the-wisps or something and leave us alone." Jade glanced uneasily into the darkness.

She asked them to pocket the moss then spent a few minutes with Brynn consulting the heavens; reading the star constellations overhead to determine their direction. It was tricky, as the sky was again partially overcast.

"OK," she finally said on a sigh. "If we're right, we should go this way." She pointed into the darkness. "What do you think, Brynn?"

The boy cocked his head, stared at the sky again for a moment then nodded in sharp agreement. "Seems about right to me. We should be into that forest we saw from the fields any time now. We'll have to be careful we don't get lost. The druids should be somewhere nearby. This is very close to where they met us when we brought Dewydd."

In strained silence, the four travellers trudged their way across the uneven fields, heading south and west through the cool night.

It was hard to tell how long they had been walking when they first heard the noises. One by one they all became aware of the sound of stealthy movement off to one side. Jade caught Phoenix's wary glance around and knew he'd heard it, too. A change in Marcus's breathing and the slight scrape of metal told her when the Roman tensed and half-drew his sword.

With a gesture, she beckoned them to gather close. "I don't think it's Romans," she whispered as they huddled around. "I'm not even sure it's human."

"Agreed." Marcus nodded.

Brynn looked up at him with huge, dark eyes.

Phoenix grimaced and drew his weapon. "If it's not human, I'm not sure I want to know what it is."

"I'll find out." Jade jerked upright and flung back the hood of her cloak with a sudden, defiant movement. She flipped her long hair back to reveal her ears and held up her moss-light close to them. In a carrying voice, she announced to the darkness, "We are friends, come to visit the druid brother of one of our companions."

There was silence. She nodded at Brynn who swallowed hard and held up his own moss-light.

"Dewydd?" His voice quavered, "it's me, Brynn. If you're there, it's ok, they're friends."

An animal made a sort of whining barking noise close by, followed by the sound of four feet padding. It stopped and, without warning, a tall, dark-clad man stepped within the circle of faint light. His face lay in the shadow of a deep-cowled hood; broad hands were clasped across his stomach. Jade regarded him apprehensively, backing away as he approached.

The man reached up and pushed back his hood to reveal a wide, joyously-grinning face that bore a striking resemblance to Brynn's. Brynn squeaked with delight and flung himself into his brother's arms. Dewydd picked up his sibling in a huge bearhug and laughed. Finally, he set the boy down and laid a hand on his head.

"You've grown, lad," he said with a fond smile.

"Aye." Brynn was obviously too glad for his usual banter.

"You're well?" Dewydd looked at the boy's thin face. "Who has had the care of you since our parents died?" He frowned at Jade and the others. "These?"

"Nay!" Brynn replied in outraged tones. "I'm big enough to look after myself, brother." He laid a hand on Jade's arm and spoke with pride. "These are my quest-companions and brothers-in-arms. We seek to—"

Jade put a hand on over his. He stopped and looked up at her in surprise.

"Careful, Brynn. You may put your brother in danger

with too much knowledge."

Brynn glanced at his brother then nodded.

"Just be assured," Phoenix added, "that we are enemies of Rome."

"And yet you walk with your enemy?" The druid sent a meaningful look at Marcus.

The Roman drew himself up tall, laying a hand on his sword and looking down at the brown-robed druid with cool hauteur. Tension pulled the air between them.

Jade stepped forward, laying a calming hand on Marcus's arm. "He is Bound to us and no threat to you, either. We trust him."

Dewydd raised his brows. "I hope your trust is not misplaced."

Turning his back on the Roman, the tall druid gave Phoenix a faint smile. "You are wise not to entrust others with your plans." He held out a hand and clasped forearms with Phoenix in friendship. "Your little band is welcome with us for the night. Come." He looped an arm around Brynn's shoulders and turned away.

Jade followed, eyeing Marcus's black scowl worriedly.

Dewydd led them into a grove of trees not far away. As they crossed beneath the boughs, the darkness thickened. Jade frowned and shook her head. She her rubbed her eyes and blinked several times.

"What is it? Romans? Druids?" Phoenix whispered, fingers curling again around the hilt of his sword.

"No, it's magic of some sort," she murmured back. "This grove is protected somehow – look!"

At her startled gasp, Phoenix glanced up and he, too, gasped.

What they had taken for a small stand of trees, now seemed to be an enormous expanse of forest. Blinding darkness had been replaced with a gentle luminescence; similar to the moss-light Jade created. Endless, ancient trunks of trees marched into the distance. Each one glowed with faint green light, giving the entire forest the appearance of being underwater.

"It's beautiful." Jade gazed about, awed.

"Aye," Dewydd said, "and it's our sanctuary in these troubled times." He pursed his lips and gave a strange, warbling whistle. "My brother druids will be coming to greet you then you will go before the Elders."

"The Elders?" Jade was uneasy. Something suddenly felt wrong. Finding Dewydd had been too simple.

Dewydd nodded. "You'll need to speak to the Elders before I can grant your request, of course."

"Errr..." Phoenix spoke for them all. "Our request?"

Dewydd bowed, looking amused. "I cannot give you the Jewel of Asgard without the Elders' permission."

Jade gasped; Marcus took a wary step backward and Phoenix half-drew his sword. Even Brynn inched away from his brother, his eyes wide with awe.

****

CHAPTER SIXTEEN

"Why do you desire the Jewel of Asgard, Warrior?"

Phoenix and the others knelt inside a small circle of glossy black stones, deep in the forest. True to his word, Dewydd had led them through the eerily-lit trees and brought them before the Council of Druid Elders. Brynn's brother had shepherded them inside the stone circle and pushed them gently to their knees before bowing and retreating outside the stones. Now, Phoenix and his companions must justify themselves and somehow convince the Druids to give up the Jewel.

If that didn't work, they would have to steal it, and Phoenix didn't like their chances of that. There was powerful magic at work in this ancient forest – even he could sense it. By the way Jade kept blinking and squinting, every stone and trunk of the place must ooze power.

He gathered his thoughts and replied to the question. He couldn't see the speaker but suspected the Elders were lurking in the shadows of the twelve tall standing stones that encircled them.

"We have been placed under a geas, good sirs," he began, trying to find the right words to impress these men of ancient power. "We must complete five quests. The first of these is to obtain the Jewel of Asgard."

"And what will you do with the Jewel if you get it?" a second disembodied voice asked.

"Our second quest requires that we take the Jewel and return it to its owner in…in the land of the Norse people, across the sea."

Phoenix was surprised to find that piece of information in his head just when he needed it. Previously, he hadn't been able to remember any details for Level Two or Three.

He caught Jade's astonished look and shrugged. Brynn's jaw dropped and Marcus frowned darkly. This was the first time their two Companions had heard where they were going next – if they managed to complete this level.

There was a long silence. Phoenix wondered if he'd said something wrong.

A third voice chimed in from behind him. "So, you do not wish to use the Jewel for the power it holds?"

"Errr..." Phoenix glanced at Jade for help. She pulled a face and shook her head. Marcus and Brynn both returned his stare blankly. "I'm sorry?" He felt like an idiot for saying it. "We didn't actually know the Jewel had a power. We just want to keep it out of the Romans' hands and return it to its owner so we can get on with the Third Quest."

This time the silence had a quality of surprise to it. He hoped that was good.

"What is the nature of your Fifth and final Quest, Warrior?" Yet another voice asked.

"We must master the Yu Dragon and defeat the Warlock, Feng Zhudai," Phoenix announced boldly, repeating what had come up on the computer when he'd first created his character.

He tried to continue, to explain that Zhudai was now helping the Romans but he was drowned out by a babble of voices from the shadows. As much as he strained to hear, the words were meaningless to him. He glanced at the others but they obviously couldn't understand the language, either. Frustrated, Phoenix grimaced and stretched his back. His knees hurt from all this kneeling.

"Enough!" The disembodied voice cut across the blether, silencing the others. "We have long known the Jewel must be returned, that is not what we must debate here. Its power is too great. We have used it for our own ends and have helped our people as much as we can against the Romans. We cannot keep it any longer lest we become exactly the sort of tyrants we fight against. Our destiny is fixed and nothing must prevent it or the balance will be disturbed. The Jewel must be sent back before it falls into Roman hands. The question we must answer is 'how'. Dewydd; take them away."

"Come!" Dewydd appeared out of nowhere beside them.

He looked troubled as he helped Jade and Brynn to their feet and led the way out of the stone circle. Around them, the voices continued what sounded like a heated argument.

"What's going on?" Phoenix asked. "Where are you taking us? Can we have the Jewel or not?"

"The Elders have heard your request and are considering it." The druid ignored Phoenix's other questions. "I will take you to where you may await the outcome of their decision."

"And what if they decide not to give it to us?" Jade demanded.

"Then your Quest will have failed." Dewydd's reply was flat and hard as stone. "Come." He continued through the dimly-lit forest, ignoring even his young brother's questions and pleas for help.

Jade, Phoenix and Marcus dropped behind slightly.

"I don't like this at all," Jade whispered. "I have a bad feeling and a whole lot of questions."

"Me neither, and me too," Phoenix agreed. "Like: how did Dewydd know we wanted the Jewel but not why we wanted it?"

"Yes," she added, "and why did our reasons cause such an uproar in the Elder Council." She glanced up at Dewydd's broad back. "I can sense there is something really bothering him but I can't tell what it is. The power here is different from Elven magic. It's blocking me." With a grunt of frustration, she waved her hand in an odd little movement. "I can't even perform the simplest spell here."

There was an edge of panic to her voice.

"Don't freak, Jade. I'm sure the Druids don't mean us any harm." Phoenix tried to reassure her. "I agree that it's all a bit weird but what can we do?"

"We wait," Marcus said imperturbably.

Phoenix winced. "You keep saying that and I really hate it."

Marcus smiled. "I know but can you think of another idea?" When Phoenix shook his head, he added, "If we can get a look at what the Jewel is and where it's kept, we might be able to come up with another plan." He clapped a hand on Phoenix's shoulder. "I don't trust these druids but we are in their hands. We must wait."

"I still hate it," Phoenix muttered.

"Here." Dewydd halted at the base of two slender beech trees. He swung an arm at the gap between the trunks. "Step through here. There are people waiting on the other side to look after you until a decision has been reached."

Phoenix felt Jade stiffen next to him. She looked with suspicion at the druid and the trees. There was a faint magical shimmer between the trunks.

"Are we prisoners?" she asked sharply.

Phoenix glanced at her in surprise then peered at the trees and back at Dewydd, trying to divine what had set her off. She and Marcus both seemed to distrust Brynn's brother.

Dewydd shook his head. "You are not our prisoners." He returned her piercing stare steadily for a few moments then looked down at his young brother. "I would like to spend some time with Brynn." He nodded at the trees. "Please step through. He will be safe with me."

"I'd rather we all stayed together," Phoenix tried to sound reasonable. Jade's unease was catching. He didn't want the party to be separated now, even by family.

Dewydd's fingers gripped Brynn's shoulders till the

tips whitened. Brynn flinched and sent a puzzled look up at his brother.

"You must go. Brynn will remain." The druid was implacable. From nowhere, two more druids appeared, big and armed with staves. They stepped forward, crowding the three toward the beech trees.

"Brynn?" Jade sent the boy a quick, questioning look.

The boy glanced uncertainly between his friends and his brother. "I'll be ok. You go in and I'll see you when you get back for the Elders' decision." He bit his lip, visibly unsure.

Jade nodded and sent one last fierce glare at Dewydd. She turned and squared her slim shoulders before stepping through the shimmering gateway. Marcus followed. Phoenix hesitated, sent Brynn a quick salute then stepped through as well. He really didn't want to but there didn't seem to be many other options.

*****

"Drop your weapons!"

With three iron spear tips burning the skin of her throat, Jade had no option. She dropped her staff and held her hands up at shoulder height, palms outward. Her brain seethed with panic and anger. They had been tricked. Behind her, she heard Marcus gasp and Phoenix swear in shock as they stepped through the portal from the druid realm.

The Druids had betrayed them.

Six Roman soldiers placed their weapons at the boys' throats and demanded surrender. Marcus and Phoenix unslung their weapons and dropped them slowly to the ground.

It wasn't like they had a choice. She fumed. At least a hundred Roman soldiers awaited their arrival at this point. Rank upon rank stood motionless, swords drawn, arrows nocked, pila at the ready. Many held burning torches aloft. In the flickering darkness, their hard, angular faces were terrifying.

Brynn! Jade felt a small spark of hope leap as she remembered the boy was still with his brother. Dewydd had chosen to protect his young brother. Perhaps, if they were very lucky, Brynn could find a way to help them.

Her heart plummeted again. Brynn was just a kid. He had no powers and no great Warrior skills. Even if he could get into the Roman camp, there was no way he could defeat a bunch of trained Roman Centurions. He was better off alive and safe with Dewydd.

"Move!"

She was shaken out of her thoughts by the prod of a spear to her ribs. The iron tip burned her skin like fire. She gasped in pain and stumbled ahead. The body of soldiers before them parted and the three companions were guided roughly into the middle of the force. Ranks closed around them and they were surrounded on all sides by a wall of points and armour. There was no possibility of escape unless they could fly.

Jade thought briefly of the magic horn given her by Aurfanon. This would definitely qualify as Dire Peril. Unfortunately, all their backpacks were now in the hands of Roman soldiers.

Oh! Her heart sank further. That included the Hyllion Bagia and all it contained – the horn, money, javelins, food and half of their travel gear. She turned her head and opened her mouth to speak to Phoenix but a pilum tip dug uncomfortably into the base of her throat: hot ice on her skin.

"No talking." A soldier growled. "My orders are to bring you in alive but just how much alive wasn't specified."

Jade swallowed and nodded. The tip withdrew and he motioned for her to keep walking. She did but the ground blurred as tears of despair and fear filled her eyes. How could they have come so far and failed now? It just wasn't fair. The end of Level One was almost in sight. She was so close to home she could almost hear her father's voice.

What would happen now? Would she be tortured or killed in this realm? If she were, what would happen back in the real world? Would it be destroyed as the old woman predicted? Right now, she would gladly swap her looks and magic for her sister's teasing and her mother's impatience - and a hug from her father! Oh, how she missed him.

More tears gathered. She clenched her teeth, trying to stay calm. Her heart thudded uncomfortably. Two salty drops spilled down her cheeks. She hung her head to hide them. It would only make things worse if the soldiers saw her as weak. She had to think. If only she were better at these things. There must be a way out of this. No matter how real the old woman said it was, this was still just a computer game. There were always ways to get out, weren't there?

Jade almost laughed at the idea – what she needed was a keyboard, a mouse and a power button. The Escape Key would be helpful, she thought whimsically. Or how about Control-Alt-Delete to just quit out of the stupid thing altogether? Yeah. She briefly derived satisfaction from the idea of all of these big, stupid Roman bullies obliterated and deleted. The moment of black humour was fleeting as fear came surging back. No. This was too real to be deleted that easily. She had to deal with this world as it was.

A short while later they were marched into a large Roman encampment. Row upon row of tents were neatly pitched around two huge, central pavilions, in the middle of a vast, rolling plain of grassland. Beads of dew from the grass soaked her feet and Jade shivered with the chill, envying the warmth promised by small campfires flickering between the tents. Flowering pink-grey light in the east told her dawn couldn't be far away. Here and there, soldiers poked dishevelled heads out of the canvas to watch them go past. It hadn't felt like a whole night had passed but perhaps time moved differently in the Druid realm, as it had in the Faery one.

Jade wondered how the Romans got ahead of them so fast. How did they know the Players were going to see the Druids? Did they know the Druids had the Jewel of Asgard? Even worse, did the Romans already have it? Was the Quest over?

Surely not. The Druids had said they couldn't let it fall into Roman hands – not that they could be trusted, really. No, if the Romans had the Jewel, why would they still be here? They wouldn't, she reasoned; they'd be out conquering the whole country, not wasting their time capturing a few fugitives. Wouldn't they?

There was no way of knowing yet, so she tried to concentrate on her surroundings. Fatigue made it difficult to think. She made an effort to examine the Roman camp, looking for an opportunity to escape either now or later.

The camp stirred as they moved through it. Guards challenged them at every turn. Cooks bustled around numerous campfires, getting breakfast ready for hundreds of troops. Jade estimated there were at least a hundred tents in the area. That had to mean at least two full Cohorts of soldiers, plus all the support staff that went with them. They can't have been in the area too long, she decided. The grass around the tents was not worn away and the smell from distant latrine areas wasn't overpowering yet. Maybe only a day or so, at a guess.

With that in mind, she had a rough idea of who they might meet when they made it to the ornate pavilions that dominated the central camp. There was only one person in this game who would go to this much trouble to catch them. Only one person who had a vested reason for moving two Cohorts of soldiers across a hundred leagues on a forced march, just to capture four people. One person who stood to lose most if they succeeded in Level One: Feng Zhudai.

Contrary to her expectations, however, they weren't

immediately led before the great wizard. Instead, they were pushed into the largest pavilion. It was furnished but unpeopled. At least twenty guards took up posts around the tent, and two inside, so escape was impossible. Trapped, the three companions stood and stared at each other.

"Umm..." Phoenix inspected the luxurious furnishings and decorations surrounding them. "This isn't exactly the prison I was expecting. Whose tent is this, do you think?"

The canvas walls were hidden by drapes of exotic-looking fabric; Persian rugs littered the floor; richly-embroidered cushions lay scattered across every seat and couch. Four main posts holding up the roof were carved with a riot of fruit and animal shapes. On a nearby, ornate wooden table, a large, gold-painted glass jug held some sort of red liquid. Four wine-glasses stood empty next to it. A massive ceramic bowl held figs, oranges, apples, pomegranates and dates. The bowl was decorated with black and gold images of Roman gods and goddesses.

Right in the centre of the back wall was a wide, low dais. Upon that sat a richly-inlaid and carved throne-like chair. A banner hung behind it, embroidered with a golden eagle with wings spread and the words:

CN IVLIO AGRICOLA LEGATO AVG PRO PR MUNICIPIVM

Jade pointed to the words, a chill settling around her guts as she mentally translated the Latin script. "Gnaeus Julius Agricola, Legate of the Emperor with pro-praetorian power." She paused, taking in the opulent surroundings again. "Somehow, I don't think it's Zhudai's tent. It must belong to the leader of these soldiers – one of Agricola's commanders, at least."

"Phoenix!" Marcus's urgent summons brought both of them to his side.

He stared at the banner. For the first time since they had known him, the Roman boy looked anxious. He laid a hand on each of them, his dark eyes intense with some emotion.

"There's something important I have to tell you."

Before he could finish, a new voice spoke pleasantly from the doorway.

"Ah! There you are Marcus; and you've brought some friends, I see."

Catching the sick, frightened look on Marcus's face, Jade spun to see this new threat.

A tall, aristocratic man stood just inside the door. He wore the dress of a Roman soldier but with much extra adornment and gilding to indicate a high rank. Over one shoulder was a soft, white drape of cloth edged with gold and purple. The helmet in his hands had scarlet plumes of feathers and more gilding. He placed it gently on a small table and advanced. His movements were that of a seasoned fighter while his voice and manners were of a civilised gentleman. The coldness of his dark eyes, however, spoke of a ruthless, intelligent man.

"So, Marcus..." He nodded slightly. "Will you introduce us or shall I do it for you?"

When Marcus simply stared at the floor in silence, the Roman smiled – but it was not a nice smile. Jade shivered as he turned it on her.

"Jade, isn't it; and Phoenix? I'm so pleased to meet you, finally. My son obviously thinks a great deal of you."

When the two did nothing but gape at him, he raised one eyebrow and shook his head in mock regret. Smoothly, he sank into the thronelike chair, leaned back and waved a hand at the banner overhead.

"Youngsters these days. Such manners. Didn't Marcus ever mention that his father was the Governor of Britannia? You'd almost think he wasn't proud of my achievements."

****

CHAPTER SEVENTEEN

Phoenix and Jade turned horrified looks on Marcus. His father was Governor Agricola – this cold, hard man in front of them? Agricola chuckled. Marcus kept his eyes on his own toes, his mouth thin, his hands gripped into tight fists.

Phoenix had a flash of recall. That was exactly how he had stood before his stepfather only a few days before in the real world. In that second of understanding, the brief flare of anger he'd felt against Marcus vanished. In its place was empathy. If this unpleasant Roman was Marcus's father, Phoenix could easily see why the boy had run away – if he really had.

That was the key question: had Marcus run away, or had he just been planted to betray them to his father? Was that how Agricola knew so much about them now? His momentary empathy vanished. He couldn't think of any other logical explanation. The Romans had known exactly where to find them and what their names were. Who else could have told them that? Anger burned again in his veins. He and Jade had taken Marcus into their group in good faith and Marcus had betrayed them to their enemies.

Phoenix slid a glance sideways at Jade. She was looking thoughtfully at Marcus. She rubbed the palm of her left hand with her right thumb. Then she looked under her lashes at Phoenix. She seemed to be trying to send him some sort of message. Her green eyes narrowed. She tilted her head a little and rolled her eyes downward.

He looked down but all he could see was her finger pointing and tapping at the palm of her left hand. What was that all about? He inspected his own left hand but saw nothing. Catching her eye again, mouthed 'what?' Jade grimaced in frustration and shook her head a fraction.

A sudden movement attracted their attention back to the Governor. He stood up. They stayed mute as he approached. He brushed past them and picked up the wine jug. In silence, he offered them a drink, shrugging when they all shook their heads. Agricola poured himself a glassful and sipped it. Over the rim, his hard eyes were thoughtful. With a voice like silk, he invited them to sit. When they continued to stand, he laughed and took the throne again, idly flipping a dagger over in his fingers.

"Where is the Jewel of Asgard?" He spoke in a pleasant tone, as though the answer was of little consequence.

Phoenix looked up in shock. How could he know to ask them about it? He cast a fulminating glance toward Marcus, torn between relief that the Romans clearly didn't have the Jewel and anger at being betrayed. Instead of catching Marcus's eye, he encountered a fierce glare from Jade that surprised him. What the...?

"Where is the Jewel of Asgard?" the Roman Governor repeated softly. He swirled the deep red wine in his glass, apparently fascinated by its colour. "If you tell me now, we can avoid a great deal of unnecessary bloodshed." He smiled again.

Jade wrapped her arms around herself and Phoenix gripped instinctively for his absent sword.

Agricola stood up and strode over to Jade. Tilting her chin up, he raised the point of his dagger to her face and pressed the flat of the iron blade against her pale cheek. She gasped and flinched away, raising a hand to her cheek. When she dropped her hand again, Phoenix saw an angry red mark there, like a burn in the shape of a blade.

Agricola sneered. "I thought so. A Faery half-breed."

Pacing in front of all three prisoners, he spoke in smooth, almost casual tones. "There is a man. Feng Zhudai. Ah! I see you know of him and of course..." He nodded at Phoenix's start then bowed politely towards his son.

"Marcus foolishly attempted to kill him not long ago." He laid a hand on his son's shoulder. Marcus jerked away.

"Zhudai will be here tomorrow." Agricola stepped in front of Phoenix and caught his eye.

Phoenix lifted his head and stared back defiantly.

Agricola leaned closer, his tone menacing. "You would be wise to tell me what I want to know. If you don't I will hand you over to Zhudai for interrogation." There was a flicker of loathing in his dark eyes. "And you truly do not want to be interrogated by that man if you can avoid it." He straightened and paced back to Jade, touching her marked cheek with the tip of his finger. "He will do much worse than that, so take this last chance and tell me where the Jewel is."

When none of the three spoke, Agricola shook his head in mock regret. "Such a pity. It doesn't really matter, though. We know that it will be in the great Stone Circle tomorrow with the druids. We'll just get it then. It may be a little more bloody than we anticipated. A great many druids will die and that will be your doing. Your choice." He cocked an eyebrow at them. "Still silent? Very well. Guards!"

Four more soldiers came in and saluted.

"Take these three to the prison tent and guard them well." Agricola eyed Jade speculatively. "Set at least thirty men outside the tent and another thirty at ten paces away. That should be sufficient against whatever barbaric powers you possess." With a sharp nod, he dismissed them.

Marcus, Jade and Phoenix silently followed the Roman soldiers through the camp. Whispers and talk followed them in turn. One soldier standing by even threw a clod of dirt at Jade and yelled something rude about her Elven blood. She flushed red but kept her head down. Phoenix, however, ignored them, feeling fractionally more hopeful than he had since they'd left the Druid realm.

There was still a chance to get the Jewel before the

Romans; still a chance to complete the Level successfully. If Agricola was right then tomorrow must be the Spring Equinox ceremony. The Jewel would be at Stonehenge with the Druids. There had to be a way to get there in time. They had to escape.

The soldiers marched them straight to a prison tent not far from Agricola's pavilion. The tent was not conveniently near the edge of camp and the sixty guards set outside were not in any danger of allowing them to easily escape. On the contrary, the Romans assigned to guard them appeared grimly keen on their duty.

Inside the small tent were just the bare essentials: three stools, three camp beds, a jug of water and a large, lidded pot. After a moment's thought, Phoenix realised it must be a chamber pot – to be used as a toilet. He screwed up his nose and dwelt for a moment on home and his private bathroom with brief longing.

All three companions slumped on either a bed or a chair without speaking. Phoenix sat with elbows on his thighs, hands and head hanging. Marcus lay on his back, staring blankly up at the canvas ceiling. After a while, Phoenix heard a noise and looked up to see Jade sitting with her hands covering her face. Slow tears leaked out from between her fingers and her body shook with sobs.

Unable to stand the sound, he moved over and put an arm awkwardly around her shoulders.

"Hey." He patted her back. "It'll be ok. We'll find a way to escape. C'mon!" He gave her a little push on the arm. "We can't quit now, we're almost there!"

Jade dropped her hands and stared at him in despair. "I know that." She sniffed and scrubbed at her face, wincing as her sleeve scraped the iron-burn there. "Don't you think I want to get out of here?" She held his gaze for a moment then looked away. "I just don't know what to do!"

"Can't you..." Phoenix waved at the tent flap and made a vaguely magical motion with his hand. "Y'know....do something to the guards?" he finished lamely.

"No." It was a flat denial. "On a good day I could probably put twenty of them to sleep." With a sniff and a tremor in her voice, she continued. "But I'm tired. I haven't slept much for two days. Plus, there are sixty of them *and* a whole camp-full beyond them. I'm useless."

"Don't belittle yourself!" Marcus's deep voice interrupted her self-criticism. He swung his legs over the side of the bed and sat up to face them. "You're far from useless. Your magic might be limited but you're smarter than anyone else I know. Agric..." He clenched his jaw and started again. "My father thinks he's got us trapped but he's underestimated us, Jade. We can think our way out of this. We have to stop him and Zhudai from getting the Jewel."

"We? What makes you think we want you to come along?" Phoenix leapt to his feet, growling at the Roman boy. "It's your fault we're in this mess!"

"My fault?" Marcus jumped up and stood toe to toe with him; dark eyes snapping with anger.

Phoenix poked him in the chest with a finger. "How did Agricola know our names? How did he know exactly where we were? How did he know about the Jewel and the Druids?" With each poke, Marcus paled and edged backward.

"You told them, didn't you?" Phoenix hissed. "You betrayed us. You spied on us and now we're here, because of you!" Seeing through a red haze of anger and pent-up frustration, Phoenix grabbed Marcus's tunic, ready to punch the living daylights out of him.

"Stop it! Stop it, Phoenix! Marcus!" Jade shoved between them, pushing Phoenix backward with surprising strength. The bed caught him behind the knees and he sat heavily, panting in anger. When Marcus tried to step around her, she gave him an ungentle shove and he, too, had to sit down.

"Marcus did not betray us, Phoenix." Jade stood with

her hands on her hips, glaring at both of them.

"How do you know?" Phoenix was scornful, certain he was right.

She thrust her left hand under his nose. "Remember the Binding spell I did?" She snatched up his hand and Marcus's and turned them palm-upwards. "If one of us betrays the others, you get a sharp pain the hand and the vine reappears, remember?" She shook their hands. "No pain, no vine. Marcus did not betray us."

Phoenix pulled his hand away and inspected it. She was right. He felt nothing. He'd forgotten about that aspect of her spell. That's what she'd been trying to tell him in the pavilion. He'd been so caught up in righteous anger, he hadn't been thinking clearly. Feeling guilty, he looked over at Marcus.

"Sorry," he apologised gruffly, "but you have to admit it's a logical thing to think."

Marcus glanced up, eyes glittering for an instant before he turned away again. His shoulders slumped.

"As much as I hate to say it, you're right." He scrubbed a hand over his face. "Even though I didn't mean to betray you, I did."

"What!?" Jade and Phoenix both yelped at the same time, fixing the Roman with hurt, disbelieving stares.

"What do you mean?" Jade demanded.

"I had forgotten one rumour about Feng Zhudai's magical powers." Marcus's reply was heavy with regret. "He has the ability to Farsee people he knows. Zhudai knows me. He must have been 'watching' me – and, of course, you – ever since we defeated that Centurion in the forest. That's how he knew to send the Cohort to us at the Dryad tree. That's how he knew we were going to talk to Dewydd and the Druids. That's how they know the Druids will be at the Circle tomorrow with the Jewel. He couldn't find you in the faery realm because I was in the Hyllion Bagia but it didn't matter because they knew where we were going." Marcus slumped forward, his head in his hands. "So it is my fault. You were right, Phoenix."

The three were silent awhile, digesting this astonishing piece of information.

"Well." Jade cleared her throat and sat down like her legs had given way. "That explains a lot."

Phoenix struggled for a moment with his anger toward Marcus. It was hard to forgive him but how could he really blame him, either? The hairs on the back of his neck prickled at the thought of previous conversations. What had they said about their goals, powers and ideas that might put them in further danger from their arch-enemy? Luckily a lot of the vital conversations he'd had with Jade had been held out of earshot of Marcus. Hopefully that had protected them a bit, anyway.

He shook himself, seeking conviction and purpose again. Whatever happened, they couldn't stay here and wait for Zhudai. If he had found out about their amulets then they needed to get away fast. The old woman in grey had specifically told them to protect the amulets. Handing themselves and their pendants over to Zhudai seemed like a really dumb move.

"So," he began, "what do we do about it? We can't stay here just waiting until Zhudai shows up tomorrow. We're too close to give up now. Isn't the Druid ceremony at dawn?" Energised by his own frustration, Phoenix paced the small tent, looking vainly for some miraculous escape route.

Nothing appeared.

"I think," Jade began then paused when the other two looked at her expectantly. "I think I might be able to do something to Marcus that will stop Zhudai from eavesdropping on us, at least."

Marcus looked apprehensive, clearly uncomfortable with the idea of more magic being performed on him.

"We could shove him back in the Hyllion Bagia,"

Phoenix suggested, only half-joking.

Marcus cast him a strait look, one brow raised in scorn.

Jade shook her head. "For starters, we don't have the bag, remember? I can't tell you what I'm going to do – for obvious reasons. I'll just have to do it."

Marcus squared his shoulders and stood up. "Well, get on with it then."

"OK." She tapped her teeth and glanced around. "Lie down on the bed with me. Phoenix, cover us completely with those blankets and don't uncover us until I say so – no matter what you see or hear. I don't want Zhudai to know what I'm doing."

Phoenix almost choked in shock. Marcus gasped, stammering out an embarrassed refusal.

Much to Phoenix's relief, Jade burst into self-conscious laughter. She blushed, shook her head and called them both idiots. The boys exchanged sheepish grins and the lighthearted episode did much to restore their friendship.

Marcus lay on the bed and Jade sat up beside him. When they were both completely draped in blankets, they looked extremely silly. Jade began to murmur soft Elvish words and Phoenix heard Marcus gasp. A faint, purple-blue light shone through the thin blankets. It seemed to be centred somewhere around his chest. As Jade continued to chant, the light travelled slowly all the way down to his toes then right back up to his head before settling again on his chest.

In less than ten minutes, it was over. Jade's form beneath the blanket slumped and Phoenix heard her draw a deep, shuddering breath. Marcus quickly cast off the covers and sat up. He caught Jade in his arms just as she collapsed sideways. The red mark on her face showed livid against her pale skin.

"Is she alright?" Phoenix dropped to his knees beside them.

Marcus slid awkwardly off the bed and they manoeuvred her onto it. Phoenix knelt on one side of her and Marcus the other. Her shadowed eyes were closed, her face white and drawn.

"What did she do to you?"

The Roman shook his head. "I have no idea. It just made me feel kind of cold all over. I don't feel any different now. Do I look any different?"

Phoenix inspected him. "Nope. Whatever she did it sure took it out of her." He laid light fingers on her neck and sighed in relief. "Her pulse is regular. I think she's just sleeping."

Marcus reached out and gently touched the tip of his finger to the burn on Jade's skin. "Why did my father's blade mark her so?" His eyes were full of her pain.

Phoenix thought about it. "I think iron is deadly to the Faery folk. She's only half-Elven, so it just burned her."

The Roman nodded absently, smoothing Jade's white-blonde hair back from her face before clearing his throat and moving away. He sat back on another bed and stared hard at Phoenix.

"So now what?"

"We can't really make any plans until we know what she did. We're probably pretty safe from Zhudai until he gets here tomorrow morning. We all need sleep so…" Phoenix quirked a grin. "We wait."

Marcus groaned. "Somehow I knew you were going to say that."

****

CHAPTER EIGHTEEN

It was close to dusk when Jade at last awoke. Phoenix and Marcus took turns sleeping and watching over her. Phoenix grudgingly made use of the chamber pot. Marcus was surprised at his reluctance but Phoenix couldn't imagine how to explain a flush toilet, so he didn't bother.

At noon, a soldier handed some bread and cheese through the tent flap. The boys divided it into three and saved a large portion of the water for Jade as well.

By the time she stirred, Phoenix was restless. She'd slept close to ten hours. If they were going to come up with an escape plan, it needed to be soon. Night time was their best chance of avoiding guards.

Finally she shifted, groaned and sat up. She rubbed her eyes, stretched and blinked in the gloom. "Where...? Oh." Recollection flashed across her face and she grimaced. "I remember. Marcus!" She swung her legs off the bed, squinted at the Roman boy then nodded in apparent satisfaction.

"What is it?" Phoenix murmured.

Jade waggled a hand at him. "I can see the spell I put on him like a kind of fuzzy purple aura around his body."

"What kind of spell?" Marcus asked uneasily.

"Just a variation on an Illusion spell," she replied. "I sort of tweaked it to make it deflect Farseeing. So, you're kind of like a stealth-guy, now." She smiled a little at Marcus's confused expression. "Basically, it should mean that Zhudai can't Farsee you anymore."

Shoo-ing the boys toward the front of the tent, she made use of the chamber pot.

"Tweaked?" Marcus muttered to Phoenix. "Stealth-guy? Are these some sort of arcane magic words?"

"Um...yes?" Phoenix replied. "It's a bit hard to explain. Don't worry about it."

"What was that noise?"

He jumped at the sound of Jade's voice right beside his ear. "Don't sneak up on me like that."

"Sorry. Did you hear that?" She frowned in concentration. "I'm sure I heard something out there."

Phoenix strained his ears but heard nothing beyond the normal camp-noises of people talking and laughing, pots banging and fires crackling. Marcus listened too but, eventually both shook their heads.

Jade huffed. "I'm sure I heard…I don't know, maybe chanting? No. It's stopped now…nevermind." She sat back on a stool and began to gnaw on the bread and cheese they had left her. "OK. How are we going to escape then?"

"We were kind of hoping you'd come up with something." Phoenix shrugged. "I'm more the action type."

"Surely you came up with something," she said thickly, swallowing down the food.

Phoenix raked his fingers through his hair. "Unfortunately all my ideas involved having our weapons and equipment – and there being about forty less guards; plus a lot of fog. Or even rain, at a pinch."

"Has there been any sign of Zhudai arriving?" She seemed anxious about that. "I really don't want to meet him right now. He's way out of my league!"

"League?" Marcus shook his head frowning over the slang. "He will not be many leagues away at all. My father said he would arrive tomorrow. If he were here, we would have been taken before him already."

Jade chewed slowly on the last fragment of bread, frowning. "I guess our best chance is to wait until three or four in the morning – when the guards are sleepy."

"They will be expecting that," Marcus put in.

"I know but they'll still be sleepy - or at least a bit less alert." She grimaced. "Fog would have been nice." She held up a hand at Phoenix when he opened his mouth. "No, I can't make fog. Or rain."

"Actually," Phoenix said mildly, "I was going to ask if you could do something with that Illusion spell you mentioned. Like maybe make the guards think we were going one way...what?" He trailed off as the other two looked at him in astonishment. "Stupid idea?"

"No." She blinked at him. "Quite possibly a brilliant idea! I think I can put maybe twenty of the guards on this side into a light sleep and still have enough energy to throw an illusion that should fool the others. After that we just have to make it to the edge of the forest and we can hide."

"What about our gear and weapons?" Marcus reminded them.

"Oh." She frowned. "I forgot. We might just have to leave them behind and steal weapons from the guards. We should have a Plan B in case one of us gets captured or held up, too."

The three of them discussed their escape plan in as much whispered detail as they could. There were a whole lot of ways in which things could go horribly wrong but they had to make the attempt.

Finally, Marcus and Phoenix settled down to sleep while Jade kept watch. Sometime after midnight, she woke them. The glow of campfires had died down, so the world outside was lit only by the ghostly, clear white light of the near-full moon high above. Sounds of camp talk and revelry were replaced by the occasional cough or snore as hundreds of soldiers slept. Outside their tent sounded the creak of leather and low-voiced conversations of their guards.

"They're still awake," Phoenix whispered, easing a neck muscle stiffened from sleeping on the hard pallet.

"They *are* professional soldiers," Marcus said.

Jade pulled back the tent-flap a few centimetres and peered out.

"The guards are standing in three circles around the tent." she murmured. "There are ten close to us, twenty just beyond them and thirty even further away. The first ten and the twenty are facing us but the others are facing outward."

"Can you do it?" Phoenix looked past her, into the moon-washed night outside.

"I don't know," she said. "I just wish I had my herb bag. I could use some more energy but we don't really have any other options, do we?"

The others shook their heads. Marcus laid a hand on her shoulder and squeezed gently.

"You can do this, Jade. Believe it."

She sent him a quick look of gratitude mixed with self-doubt. Taking a deep breath, she whispered final instructions. "I'm going to try and put a group of twenty on this side into a light trance-sleep so they will look like they're still awake and standing up. Then I'll throw the illusion of us running the other way to draw off the rest. Ready?"

"One problem," Phoenix muttered. "We can't see in the dark like you can."

"It's almost a full moon. It's as bright as day. You should be fine."

"Fair enough." He nodded once. He'd feel better once he had a sword in his hand, that was certain.

"OK." Jade spoke one soft word in Elvish and a kind of heaviness swept through the tent. Phoenix blinked, feeling the weight of her sleep spell brush him. She swayed a little. Marcus steadied her as she murmured again and pointed a finger toward the back of the tent.

For a second, he thought he saw three ghostly figures turn and run through the canvas. Marcus gasped and shivered. Jade sagged between them, stumbled and recovered.

"Now!" she whispered harshly, shaking off their hands and hauling open the tent flap.

A hoarse cry went up from the guards around the side of the tent. For a moment, Phoenix thought they'd been seen but the sound of movement, yelling of orders and silhouettes of dark figures showed the guards rushing away from the tent opening. They were following Jade's illusion people. The plan was working.

The three took several stealthy steps before almost colliding with the first sleeping guard. It was unnerving to see him standing, wide-eyed and motionless right in front of them. Phoenix had to snap shut his teeth to hold back a yell. His breath clouded in the cold night air. He managed to keep his wits enough to quickly slide two Romans' swords out of their sheaths. Marcus followed suit, relieving two other soldiers of their weapons. Phoenix hefted the gladii, feeling their strange weight and shape, wondering if he could use them effectively. They were several inches shorter than the weapon he normally carried and had no hand guard.

Jade tugged on his arm. "I can only hold both spells for a few minutes. Let's go!"

Phoenix nodded and threaded his way through the guards toward what he hoped was roughly north. From Brynn's descriptions of Salisbury Plain in 80AD, he was pretty sure Stonehenge would lie west and maybe a little south of this Roman encampment. It shouldn't be too far away, either. They had decided, though, it would be safer to try and return to the Druid forest sanctuary. Hopefully they could get Brynn and the Jewel of Asgard before the dawn ceremony commenced – and that meant going northeast again.

The sound of guards chasing illusions roused other soldiers. All around, men in tents were asking sleepy questions and gathering weapons. Any second now, dozens of tent flaps would fly open and hundreds more soldiers would join the fray. The three escapees began to run in earnest.

They cleared the tents and raced toward the perimeter guards. Dozens of men stood in a loose circle around the camp. Some faced outward, watching for danger. Others peered inward, trying to understand the chaos happening inside the camp. Many held torches aloft. They must have been ordered to stay put and hold the perimeter but they were clearly hoping to get some action.

Jade grabbed his arm and Marcus's. "Don't start anything, if you don't have to. We all have to get through if we can, remember?"

Phoenix nodded curtly. It was a nice idea but he had a feeling they weren't going to be able to just waltz through the perimeter unchallenged. In a way, he preferred to stand and fight. He was tired of all this walking, talking, hiding and running away. He was a warrior. Fighting was what his character did best.

Sure enough, as they got nearer, the first soldiers stepped up and called out a command to halt and be recognised. The three kept running. More soldiers gathered. Phoenix glanced across at Jade and Marcus.

"There's no way we'll all be able to sneak through now. Time for Plan B!" he yelled at Jade.

She and Marcus looked at each other and nodded. Jade fell back a few steps, letting the two warriors take the lead. Phoenix didn't see what happened to her next. He was too busy heading into battle in order to give her a chance to slip past. Holding a sword in each hand, he ran full-tilt at the nearest soldiers. It was time for action.

With a bloodthirsty yell, Phoenix fell on the enemy. His swords darted and flickered as he let his Warrior instincts take over. With a clang, one blade met an opponent's. The collision jarred up into his shoulder. He disengaged, deflected a second fighter's jab with his other sword and twisted away from both. Now three closed in on him, calling out instructions to each other. Another tried to slip behind but Marcus appeared, protecting his back.

"Where's Jade?"

The Roman parried two thrusts with a grunt. "She made it through the lines and has gone for the Druids, as we planned."

"Well," Phoenix growled, "let's hold them as long as we can and hope Jade can find Brynn and they can convince the Druids to help. Otherwise, this could be a very short fight. Why she thinks they'll help when they betrayed us, I don't know!"

"We don't have a lot of other choices," Marcus replied grimly.

There was no more time for talk. The pair fought on. Phoenix caught a blow on his forearm, glad the Romans hadn't taken his leather and iron armguards. As it was the force of it almost numbed his fingers. For several frightening seconds he could barely grasp the sword. He lashed out with a kick to escape being skewered.

He stepped a little away from Marcus then realised the soldiers were trying to separate them and moved back. Behind him, Marcus's heavy breathing and the slicker and clash of metal told him the Roman boy still fought strongly. They couldn't afford to let anyone between them. The only reason they weren't dead already was that the Romans couldn't all get close at once. There were only ever three or four near enough to trade blows at any one time. If they got smart enough to back off and let the archers loose, though...

Desperation crept into Phoenix's heart little by little. His arms slowed; the muscles starting to burn. His breath came in short gasps. Metal clanged again as he barely turned aside a jab aimed at his stomach. Five Romans were down at his feet; three dead and two badly wounded but more stepped into the gaps. He wasn't going to last much longer at this rate. Plus, he was at a disadvantage. He wasn't used to working with gladii and they were.

He had to change tactics. Just being a barbarian warrior wasn't going to cut it. He had to do something new.

Drawing a deep breath, he opened the part of his mind that held his aikido experience. There had to be a way to get this body to use both skills. He watched how his opponents moved, conserving his energy to deal with truly lethal attacks, rather than bluffs. Deliberately, he made his footwork more circular, more like aikido movements. It was difficult. His 80AD body-memory kept trying to revert to chop-and-hack. Phoenix clenched his teeth, focussing all his will on the basic concept of aikido - blending. Only this time it was not an opponent he had to blend with - it was himself: his two minds and fighting styles. This had to work, or they were dead.

A window opened in his mind, understanding flooded in. His body responded, moving as he wanted it to; his two styles of fighting seemlessly merging and under his full control. His movements became flowing, circular, his sword work more like that of a Samurai.

It was a brilliant move. These particular Romans had clearly never fought against an Eastern style of swordplay. It confused them. They had no idea what to expect from his concise, centred movements. With a series of well-timed, well-placed blows, Phoenix sliced five soldiers from neck to torso or from side to side. The others fell back, stunned by the ferocity of his attack.

Behind him, Phoenix heard Marcus's breath coming quick and deep.

"You OK?" he called anxiously.

"Not...for much longer," Marcus managed.

"I know." Phoenix's heart sank as more soldiers crowded behind the ones now eyeing them with open hostility. "I'm sorry I got you into this and I'm honoured to have known and fought with you, Marcus."

"And...you," the Roman boy replied between white breaths. "Die well, friend."

"Frankly," Phoenix muttered as the soldiers moved in again, "I'd rather not die at all but we don't seem to have much say in it."

Marcus gave a short laugh as his sword came up to block a blow at his head.

Their opponents surged forward with renewed determination. Phoenix now blended his two sword styles to cause the most confusion possible. It worked for a while but his strength drained away like water. More and more strikes came close to his body. He bled from several small slices. He stumbled and barely managed to deflect a lethal cut to his throat.

Just as his weary mind and body were at the point of complete collapse, he felt an odd surge of strength. It flowed like warm honey into his exhausted muscles, seeming to ooze into his body from the outside. Not questioning his bizarre good fortune, he plunged back into the fray. Fighting with renewed vigour he ducked beneath a wild thrust to skewer another opponent.

Things got even stranger. His enemies slowed. He could see clearly every blow about to fall; anticipate the next strike from the corner of his eye; slide easily out of the way of a thrown pilum. As he watched, bewildered, they grew yet more sluggish. It was truly uncanny: as though the world had slowed down or he had sped up to super-speed.

He'd almost decided he really had developed some kind of super abilities, when the soldiers ceased all movement.

Stunned, Phoenix straightened and stared about. OK, he couldn't be that fast. All around stood a freaky tableau of frozen motion. Lit by the red glow of slow-flickering torches, snarling soldiers held swords upraised; one man had his arm drawn back to throw a pilum; an officer shouted silent orders. Dozens of men stood behind them, their faces distorted as they screamed noiseless encouragement. All as still as statues.

Movement caught Phoenix's eye and he spun, sword ready. It was only Marcus, turning circles. His eyes were wide and wild as he ducked beneath a sword and came to Phoenix's side.

"What the…?" He was breathing hard. Blood from a cut on his thigh dripped steadily into the dust.

Phoenix reached out and touched the hand of one of the soldiers. It was warm. The man rocked a little but didn't spring to life.

"I'm thinking…magic of some sort," Phoenix said. "Jade must be around somewhere. I didn't think she was this strong, though." He peered past the crowd of soldiers, toward the camp. He couldn't hear anything from beyond the circle of angry faces. Distant firelight showed dozens of figures silhouetted like still shadow-puppets in front of the orange glow. The frozen-zone seemed to extend throughout the Roman camp.

"Let's get out of here," Marcus said. He snatched a cloak from the officer and tore it into shreds. With it he bound the wound on his thigh. Phoenix did the same with the worst of his own injuries then looked around.

"How do we get through?" He indicated the solid wall of bodies between them and anywhere else. He didn't fancy trying to crawl between their legs.

Marcus smiled wickedly. "Ever played at ninepins?"

****

CHAPTER NINETEEN

"Ninepins?" Phoenix laughed. He'd never heard of it but could guess what it must be. He reached for the nearest motionless man. A gentle shove in the right direction and the Roman toppled over like a tin toy soldier. He knocked into the person nearest, who fell and in turn collided with his neighbour. Then, just like dominoes, the soldiers encircling Phoenix and Marcus teetered and fell into one another. One by one, with soft, fleshy sounds and heavy thuds, the wall of men toppled and became a heap.

The falling swelled into waves moving in circles away from the two warriors in the middle. Phoenix & Marcus watched in awe as soldiers dropped like cut wheat. Soon though, the bodies were spaced too far apart; the domino effect slowed and eventually stopped. The boys stood in the centre of what looked like a crop circle of flattened people. Swords, legs and arms stuck up at odd angles.

After exchanging an uneasy look, the companions walked where they could and climbed over the soft bodies where they couldn't find the ground. It was a very strange experience. They were profoundly glad when they could at last weave their way through standing men past the edge of the camp.

Stopping in a clear area, Phoenix peered into the shifting, moonlit shadows. Jade had to be around here somewhere.

"Which way?" Marcus asked. The silent Roman camp behind them was eerie. They both wanted to put space between them and it.

"To Carega Amgarn, of course," a voice piped up from nearby.

Phoenix felt a big grin split his face. Marcus's eyes lit

up.

"Brynn?" Phoenix squinted into the gloom. "Is that you?"

The Breton boy stepped into the moonlight. "In the flesh." He grinned. When Phoenix reached out to envelope him in a rough hug, the boy held out his hands and screwed up his nose. "Not until you've had a bath, thanks!"

Phoenix looked down at his blood and sweat-spattered self and had to laugh.

"Coming from you, that means I must smell bad. Where's Jade?" he demanded, "and how did you two do this?" He swept a hand at the still and silent Roman camp.

Brynn grabbed his arm and tugged. "C'mon. Jade met us coming to get you. She and Truda have gone to Agricola's tent to get your gear back."

"She met 'us'?" Phoenix latched onto the first part. "Who's 'us' and who's Truda?"

There was movement behind Brynn. A dozen or more Druids stepped forward, lowering their hoods. Dewydd led, his expression contrite. Phoenix turned toward him with a growl but Brynn jumped between them.

"No!"

"They sent us into a trap!" Phoenix snarled.

"That was all negotiated before the Elders spoke with you," Dewydd said humbly. "The Elders were simply trying to stop the Romans from destroying us; delaying them long enough so we could return the Jewel and keep it out of their hands. We didn't realise what your Quest entailed. We thought you were simply criminals the Romans were trying to recapture." Brynn's brother bowed his head. "I represent the Elders in expressing our deepest regrets. We came to rescue you as soon as a decision had been reached."

Phoenix stared at him. "You did all this?" He waved a hand back at the soldiers. Dewydd nodded, his face serene.

"How?" The scope of it was dumbfounding.

"It's complicated magic. It won't hold long, though, and we don't really have time to explain right now." There was the merest flicker of a superior grin on the druid's mouth. "We must get you all to the Stone Circle in time for the Dawn Spring Equinox ceremony. The Ceremony will allow you to complete your Quest here and get the Jewel of Asgard away from the Romans."

"But what about Jade?" Phoenix grabbed Dewydd's arm as the other turned away. "And where is the Jewel?"

"I have already given the Jewel into Jade's keeping." The druid pointed. "And she is coming up behind you now."

Sure enough, within seconds, Jade joined them. With her was a young girl about Brynn's age. She helped Jade to carry their equipment and weapons. As she handed Phoenix his sword and shield, she gave him a friendly smile, showing even, white teeth and clear blue eyes. Fiery red hair was tightly bound in two long braids down to her waist. She wore a cowled robe like the Druids' and Dewydd greeted her with a gentle smile.

Phoenix was about to ask who the heck she was, when Dewydd turned away and strode into the night without another word. Jade followed, with Brynn, the girl and the other Druids. Marcus and Phoenix exchanged confused looks and trailed behind. Belatedly, Phoenix realised the redheaded girl must be this Truda, Brynn had mentioned.

Dismissing her as irrelevant, he concentrated on following the others without tripping. Clouds scudded across the moon and the ground was dewy and uneven. Add to that his own weariness from the fight and he was bound to fall on his face if he wasn't careful.

Marcus moved alongside and sent him a speculative glance.

"Good fight," he murmured.

Phoenix nodded. A savage grin crept over his mouth as he remembered. It had felt good. They had run away from danger too often on this trip. The fight had been somehow...satisfying. He'd managed to resolve the split in his mind over which fighting style to use. Now he could use both, or either at will. It was so cool. His grin widened. This was what he'd started this game for – adventure; excitement; fun.

Abruptly, he was swept by guilt. Fun? Killing people for fun? At the beginning of this adventure he had been sickened by the idea of killing – even though he'd believed, logically, that this was a game and these people were only digital ghosts. After meeting the old woman he wasn't so sure of that, yet he'd run into that fight like the most bloodthirsty war monger in history and he'd enjoyed it! Not the killing, he realised but the adrenalin rush of the fight itself. If these people were truly real, what sort of monster did that make him?

Not a monster. Just a gamer; a survivor.

But at what cost? Where was the "do the right thing" ethic he'd discovered only a day or so ago? Was the Warrior stronger than his father's influence and his Sensei's example after all? As individuals, each one of those soldiers had done nothing to deserve death, digital or not.

He was revolted by his own actions. The memory of those deaths rose in his mind, lingering. Over and over the soldiers died in front of him. He heard their screams until he thought he was going to throw up.

"What troubles you?" Marcus gripped his arm, drawing him back to the reality he was living now. Phoenix sent him a worried look.

"I killed at least eight of them." He ground his teeth to prevent bile rising.

Marcus raised his brows and sent him a 'so?' kind of look. "And I killed six. It was us or them."

"But was it the right thing to do?" Phoenix pleaded, hoping to be absolved.

"It was the only thing we could have done," Marcus replied firmly. "They died an honourable, soldier's death. There is nothing to be ashamed of. I don't understand why you're distressed. We are at war."

Phoenix looked away. Surely there must have been another, less deadly, way of escaping if he'd really tried to find it. He'd rushed straight in, eager for battle, blood and thrills. He'd let his father, his Sensei and himself down. Now he was going to pay the price. Those soldiers' agonised faces would haunt his sleep.

"Hey, Marcus!" Jade's hail interrupted his thoughts and Phoenix was grateful for it.

"I thought you might like to know that I tipped an entire jug of wine over your father's head and stuck a grape up his nose while he was frozen."

Marcus stared at her in shock for a moment. Then, to the amazement of everyone who knew him, his calm face lit up in a smile of the most unholy delight. Brynn giggled. Marcus grinned more widely then he too began to chuckle. Before long, all four companions were laughing hard, holding their sides and hugging each other in relief.

It was several moments before Dewydd could bring their attention back to the matter at hand and get them moving again.

"Thanks for rescuing us – again." Phoenix smiled wryly at Jade, pushing his darker thoughts aside.

She smiled back, a hint of respect in her eyes. "You guys seemed to be doing pretty well on your own against a hundred or so soldiers. I just figured I should get the heck out of there while I could and leave you to it."

"Sure you did." Phoenix refused to rise to her teasing.

"It was Plan B, after all. Anyway," she added diffidently, "it's Dewydd and the others who did the magic-freezy trick. Brynn had already convinced them to come to our rescue."

"Remind me to thank both of them later."

"You may not have time." Jade pointed ahead.

Dimly, Phoenix could just make out silhouettes of the massive standing stones of Stonehenge not far away. A faint grey light coloured the eastern sky. It was close to dawn. Dewydd had said they needed to be at the stone circle before the Spring Equinox ceremony was completed. Why, Phoenix didn't know. He still wasn't even sure what an Equinox was but he was willing to go on faith for the moment, too tired to do much else. So the weary group picked up their pace until they were almost running across the plain.

The group arrived from the northeast, topping a slight rise just as the first pinks of sunrise began to colour the sky. Phoenix had never actually been to Stonehenge in his own time and he was awestruck by the sheer majesty of the structure. Not only were the stones massive but all of them were in place, just as they had appeared in the hologram shown by their amulets. Jade clutched at Phoenix's arm and the two stopped for a moment, both stunned by the timeless strength and majesty of the scene before them.

The clouds cleared. The moon had almost set. Overhead and in the west the last few stars sparkled dimly in a washed purple sky. Stonehenge stood magnificently alone in the middle of the plain, its outer ring of enormous grey sarsen stones beginning to catch faint hints of pink.

There were thirty of them; each one four metres high and two wide. Set in a massive circle, every stone was joined to the next by a perfectly-fitted lintel stone lying atop. Within that circle, Phoenix could just make out the inner circle of shorter bluestones. Inside that was a horseshoe of five groups of three huge stones - two vertical and one atop in each set. They looked like five giant doorways. Finally, mirroring those, was a horseshoe setting of more bluestones.

Phoenix glanced at Jade but her gaze was fixed on the great circle. She squinted and blinked at it, tilting her head this way and that. He knew what that meant.

"Magic?"

She nodded. "Lots. I can...kind of...see people inside. Druids, I think."

Phoenix stared but to him Stonehenge seemed empty. He gave up, taking her word for it. "We should get a move on then."

Just as he said it, Dewydd waved them forward urgently. The entire group began to run the last few hundred metres to the sacred site, their breath puffing in the cold morning air. Phoenix grinned even though his legs ached. They were nearly there. A few more minutes and they would have confounded Agricola and Zhudai and be into the next level of the Game.

He wasn't quite sure why they had to be involved in the Spring Equinox Ceremony but everyone else seemed to believe it was vitally important, so he figured it must be. Heck, if all they had needed was the Jewel, and Jade had that, then surely the Quest was over. So if it wasn't then logic said they needed to take one more step. Hopefully this druid ceremony was it.

As if sensing his confusion, Jade slipped in beside him and gave a quick explanation.

"The Vernal Equinox..." She stopped as he blinked at her in mystification. "OK, the Spring Equinox then, is the day when the sun rises right over the Equator. It means spring is definitely here and winter is over. So the Druids thank the Goddess. They celebrate the rebirth of the Earth, animals and plants, and the land's readiness for planting of summer crops and stuff." She added as an afterthought, "It was the original Easter celebration, really."

"O...K..." he puffed as they ran. "I'm not sure I needed to know that but thanks anyway."

She rolled her eyes. "Honestly." She jogged ahead, clearly annoyed that he wasn't interested in her history lecture.

Phoenix sighed. He couldn't help it if she was a walking encyclopaedia and he wasn't.

He glanced around. Marcus had fallen behind. The wound on his leg must be giving him trouble. Phoenix slowed down and waited. Ahead, Dewydd ushered his fellow druids, Jade, Brynn & Truda beneath the gigantic sarsen stone ring. Even though he'd sort of expected it, Phoenix still found it unnerving when they all vanished as they passed beneath the lintel stones. Dewydd stayed and waved at them to hurry up. Panting and limping, Marcus caught up with him and the two joined the druid.

"We must hurry." Dewydd urged.

"Yeah," Phoenix nodded, "I can see it's almost dawn but Marcus is hurt and I'm not leaving him behind." He hooked the Roman boy's arm over his own shoulder and took some of his weight. Marcus grunted thanks, his face pale and set.

"He's not the problem." Dewydd pointed back the way they had come. "They are."

The boys turned to look – and groaned. Sweeping down the hill, was a wall of scarlet and leather: soldiers. It seemed like most of the Roman encampment had turned out en force to recapture the fugitives.

"They've seen us," Phoenix yelled. "Will your magic keep them out?"

Dewydd shook his head. "It's only an illusion that prevents people seeing inside the stone circle. We cannot be cut off from the Earth by a shield at this moment. It's a time to celebrate our connection to the world, not isolate ourselves. If we raise a shield the ceremony won't work and the portal you must pass through will not open. Your quest would be incomplete and you would be recaptured." He looked gravely at the two boys. "You cannot allow the Jewel of Asgard to fall into the hands of the Romans or Feng Zhudai. They would have too much power and the Balance and Harmony of the Earth would be disrupted."

Phoenix snapped a quick frown at the druid, remembering the Yin-Yang, Balance and Harmony amulet he and Jade wore. Could it be just a co-incidence or had the Druid said something significant?

"How much time do we have?" Marcus asked through gritted teeth.

"Our people will do what they can to keep the Romans outside the circle," the druid replied. "The Elders have begun the ceremony. You must stay together. Phoenix!" Dewydd thrust a small, cloth-wrapped item into his hand and closed his fingers over it. "Use this when the time comes. Give it to whoever asks for the Jewel. It will buy you enough time to escape through the portal, if you need it. Brynn will show you the portal, when it opens." As he spoke, he pushed them between the stones.

Bemused, Phoenix tucked the small parcel into the front of his shirt and hurried on.

Inside, he spared little time on being surprised by the number of brown-robed druids milling about. There seemed to be hundreds and many carried quarterstaves and clubs. A path opened. Phoenix helped Marcus through the respectful crowd to where Jade and the others stood, loosely encircling a large altar stone.

She cast them a concerned look but he waved her back. There simply wasn't enough time to heal them and he doubted she had the energy right now anyway. Several of the Elders nodded regally in acknowledgement as the companions reunited.

At the altar, an ancient druid chanted something unintelligible. He turned and faced east, toward the rising sun. His voice rose and fell like the sea. Phoenix could almost taste the purple-blue tzing of magic in the air. His whole body began to hum and he felt the insane urge to take his shoes off and dig his toes into the soft earth beneath. He thought he could actually feel grass growing under his boots. Each breath of morning air seemed to taste sweeter than the last; a dawn chorus of birdsongs swelled to fill the sky.

Jade's eyes were wide with awe. Marcus drew a surprised breath and ducked out from beneath Phoenix's arm. Glancing down in amazement, Phoenix noticed the ground was now carpeted with flowers of every sort, with more opening each second. The young girl, Truda, bent down, patted the ground like it was a sleeping puppy then calmly picked dozens of blooms and laid them on the altar like an offering. He felt a tug on his sleeve and saw Marcus pointing to his wounded leg. Phoenix raised his eyebrows in surprise. The deep thigh slice had healed into a thin, white scar. Inspecting themselves, the two fighters realised all of their injuries were similarly cured.

Just as the first, shimmering sliver of sunlight peeked above the horizon, the ancient druid's chant became a shouted, joyous song of life. As he raised his arms, his cry was echoed by hundreds of deep voices and hundreds of lifted arms all around them. Phoenix felt a kind of soft explosion thump through his body and radiate outward from the stone circle. In the distance, even the Roman soldiers staggered as it passed through their ranks.

From the corner of his eye, he noticed the space between the largest set of three sarsen stones quiver and shine like the surface of liquid. As he tried to make sense of what it might mean, Brynn grabbed at his arm.

"There!" He pointed excitedly at it. "That's the portal. Quick!" He dragged Phoenix forward. "It'll only stay open a short time. If we miss it the chance won't come again until the Autumn Equinox."

"But the Jewel!" Phoenix protested.

"We have it," Jade answered. "Come on!"

The companions were moving toward the portal when, in a horrible parody of that worshipful druid chant, the Roman horde fell upon the druids with a bloodcurdling battle cry.

****

CHAPTER TWENTY

Phoenix hesitated, looking back at the battle. He wasn't going to abandon the Druids to their deaths. They were vastly outnumbered and carried blunt weapons against a field of swords, arrows and pila. They wouldn't last ten minutes.

Even as he reached for his sword, a flash of light and a loud *crack* echoed across the plain. After a moment of stillness, two of the enormous outer Sarsen stones toppled outward in frightful slow motion. When they and their lintel stone struck the ground, it was like an earthquake. The shock wave smacked into Phoenix's chest and shook the earth beneath his feet. Everyone staggered. There was a brief hiatus in the fighting as another stone teetered and those nearest stopped to judge its fall. With hoarse, warning yells, Romans and druids alike jostled to run from it.

Phoenix saw who was responsible – the same ancient druid who had performed the Spring rite stood atop the altar stone. He pointed at another Sarsen. Another flash of light exploded at the base and it, too toppled. The old druid clutched at his breast. With a choked cry, he collapsed on the altar. A Roman arrow protruded from his heart. The magic he had performed still took its toll. More massive standing stones fell, just like the domino effect he and Marcus had caused earlier.

Stunned, Phoenix realised what he was seeing: he and Jade caused the destruction of Stonehenge. When it was over, there would be only seventeen of the thirty outer stones left standing.

A cry from his left drew his attention. Dewydd and a group of druids fought for their lives against a dozen Romans, with more coming up behind. Phoenix raced toward them, drawing his sword and unslinging his shield in one smooth move. Uttering a wild, wordless shout, he sprang off a fallen stone and attacked the Romans from behind. Three quick slashes dropped three soldiers. A fourth man thrust wildly. Phoenix turned the gladius aside with his shield and slid his own blade underneath the overlapping armour plates on the man's breast. The soldier gasped and sagged to his knees. Phoenix pulled the edge free and turned to face his next opponent, baring his teeth in a growl.

Marcus appeared by his side, ready again to fight with him. Phoenix grinned at him. The Roman nodded back.

Dewydd cracked a soldier over the head with calm efficiency, shoving the body into his sword-mates so they stumbled and tripped over each other. Phoenix reached his side and mock-saluted.

"Want some help?"

The druid frowned at him. "No! Get out of here. Get the Jewel and my brother through the portal."

"No way." Phoenix shook his head, ducking under a swinging sword and chopping at the arm that wielded it. "I'm not leaving you lot to die."

"Noble but stupid," Dewydd growled. "You *have* to leave us. Our whole task is to make sure the Jewel is kept out of Roman hands. If the Governor gets hold of it, not only Albion will fall but this entire world will be lost and yours as well. Leave. Now."

Phoenix paused in mid-stroke, staring at the druid in astonishment. "*My* world? What? How..."

He didn't get to finish the sentence. Another gladius descended toward his head and he had to focus on not being killed.

Dewydd grunted. "Look around. The day is lost whether you stay or go. You cannot change that but you can change your own destiny."

Phoenix spared the rest of the field a glance. He was

right. Everywhere the distinctive scarlet and leather Roman uniforms overwhelmed the paltry few brown-robed druids left standing. He despatched another soldier with ruthless anger. It wasn't fair!

Brynn's brother grabbed his arm. "You must go! Take the Jewel and get through the portal before it closes. If you miss it you won't be able to leave until the Autumn solstice and that will be too late. Hurry, the Jewel is in danger. You must protect her."

"Her?!" Phoenix looked wildly around.

The druid nodded toward the portal. Near it, Jade, Brynn and half a dozen druids fought valiantly. They formed a protective circle. In its centre, Phoenix caught a flash of red hair.

"Truda?" He blocked a dagger-strike and parried a pilum jabbed at Marcus's back. "Truda is the Jewel? Are you kidding me?"

He eyed the young red-headed girl with shock. Truda was the Jewel of Asgard? Whose idea was that? He'd expected a gemstone – something easy to carry. What the heck were they supposed to do with kid to coddle and babysit? Dammit.

A thunderous *crack* made him jump. From Dewydd's hand shot a flare of greenish electricity. Roman soldiers flew through the air to land in broken, scarlet heaps, clearing a path back to Jade and the others. The druid laid a hand on Phoenix's arm.

"I can only do that once. Go. Please. Take Brynn with you."

Phoenix glanced at Marcus.

The Roman nodded solemnly. "You know I would fight with you to the death but the druid is right. We have to remember the end we all desire - Feng Zhudai."

It was true. Staying here couldn't be his decision alone. If he didn't go, they'd all suffer the consequences of his choice. Phoenix had to do what was right for all of them and for both worlds, not just what he wanted.

With a growl of frustration, he turned away. Together, he and Marcus ran through the fallen, back to their companions. Jade cast him a look of pure relief and desperation.

"Let's go then." He had to yell over the noise of the battle; had to grit his teeth against the desire to fling himself headlong back into the fray.

As a group, they edged toward the shimmering portal. The remaining druids covered their retreat, falling and dying with Roman arrows quivering in their chests.

Phoenix raised his shield. More shafts thunked into the wood. He lowered it and chopped the ends off, glaring. It wouldn't hurt to stay a little longer and take out just a few more of these guys, surely?

The choice was taken out of his hands. A large contingent of Roman soldiers swarmed through the remaining druids, encircling the Players and the few surviving Druids with frightening speed and efficiency.

They were cut off from the Door.

His hesitation had cost them the Game.

As fifty or more swords and pila pointed at their hearts, the deep sound of a horn whooped out thrice across the stone circle, echoing strangely among the rocks. Those Romans still fighting fell back to the perimeter stones and formed a solid barricade of armour and weapons. Inside the circle, bodies lay thick on the ground. The few remaining druids stumbled toward the portal, trying to regroup for the next attack.

There were no more attacks. The Roman soldiers simply stood, shoulder to shoulder, rank upon rank, waiting.

The five young travellers stood within a circle of steel, weapons drawn. Truda, they thrust into the middle of their own little defensive barrier, protecting her as best they could. The portal shimmered, just out of reach behind the

Roman line surrounding them.

They waited - but not for long.

There was a stir amongst the Romans standing between two of the sarsen stones. They parted and let someone through. Marcus clenched his fists. Agricola strode arrogantly into the circle, scarlet cape billowing in the dawn breeze, hair still damp from Jade's dousing. He glanced with indifference at the carnage before sending his son a cool smile. Picking his way between the bodies, the Roman Governor made his way up to the little group of survivors and stood, surveying them with calm hauteur.

"Give me the Jewel." His pleasant voice was at odds with the scene around them. It sounded like he was politely requesting a drink at a bar.

"Come and get it," Phoenix snarled.

Agricola shrugged. "Give me the Jewel and I will spare your lives."

Phoenix raised his eyebrows. "Somehow, I find that hard to believe."

Agricola lost a little of his cool. Glaring, he shoved his way through the line of men until he was within a few feet of the defiant group. He stood over Phoenix, aristocratic face stiff with anger.

"Alright. Give it to me now or I will have you all slaughtered – including my treacherous son and these children." He eyed the group contemptuously. "And I will find it on your dead bodies!"

Agricola didn't know. He actually didn't know the Jewel was Truda. Agricgola still thought, as they had, that the Jewel it was a thing.

Phoenix remembered the little packet given to him by Dewydd. Now it all made sense.

Wishing there was some way to warn the others, Phoenix allowed his shoulders to slump and his head to drop. "Alright," he tried to sound defeated. "You win. Let us go and you can have it."

Behind him, Jade gasped. Marcus reached out and dug his fingers into Phoenix's arm.

"What are you doing? He won't keep his word," the boy muttered.

Phoenix twisted free, trying to convey a message in the glare he turned on his friends.

"I know what I'm doing. Remember what Dewydd said? This is the only way to save ourselves."

Marcus's expression cleared to understanding. He stepped back.

"Jade." Phoenix frowned at her, flicking a quick glance down at Truda then over at the glimmering portal. "Just be ready."

Reaching slowly into his shirt, he drew out the small packet and revealed it to his friends. Jade and Brynn looked confused then tried to hide it as they caught on. He hoped Agricola hadn't seen their expressions or the deception would be over. Jade took hold of Truda's hand and pulled her close. Marcus laid a hand on Brynn's shoulder. The younger boy nodded.

With a deep sigh of regret, Phoenix turned back to the Governor. "Here then, take it."

Five guards held sword tips at Phoenix's throat as he reached out, dropped the packet into Agricola's hand and backed away again.

Marcus moved up to stand beside Phoenix. "Look." He pointed outside the devastated circle of standing stones, to the horizon beyond. In the distance, a group of horsemen galloped toward the Carega Amgard. "The flag. The red bird on a black background."

Phoenix spotted it whipping over the head of the lead rider. "What about it?"

He switched his gaze back to the Romans. The archers drew back their strings; arrows aimed at Phoenix's party.

"It's Zhudai's personal guard," Marcus murmured. "He comes."

Phoenix swore long and inventively. There were five hundred Romans between them and their arch-nemesis. They had but moments to live and absolutely no way of getting close to him alive. Even worse, they couldn't get away, either.

Eager and triumphant, the Governor of Britannia laughed. Parcel in hand, Agricola turned away with a swirl of his cloak and held the parcel high above his head. A great cheer swept through his army.

"I have it! Now we will triumph!" he shouted.

Another cheer erupted. Agricola shouldered his way back through his men. Glancing back, he gestured at his son to join him. Marcus returned his look stonily and didn't move.

"Very well." Agricola shrugged and nodded to his captain, his fingers busy with the outer coverings on the packet in his hands. "Kill them all."

The Romans advanced, spears levelled and arrows nocked.

"Now?" Jade's frightened whisper reached his ears. Phoenix shook his head.

"I don't think…"

There was a blinding flash of reddish light; a hoarse scream; shouts from Agricola's men as they tried to reach their fallen commander; confusion and fear amongst the soldiers as smoke billowed in all directions. The rank of men surrounding the companions wavered and broke as they ran to see what new threat had attacked their Governor.

"Now!" Phoenix yelled.

As one, the little group turned and sprinted for the portal.

Half a dozen stalwart soldiers still guarding the structure stood their ground, trying to prevent their escape and carry out their last order to kill. Phoenix used his momentum to full advantage. He turned aside one blade and shoulder-charged the soldier carrying it. The man stumbled, falling into his nearest shield-mate. Turning, Phoenix lashed out at the next man, catching the blade with his own sword and stabbing with his dagger. The soldier folded over the little blade with a look of surprise then slid to the ground without a sound.

Hampered by her need to keep Truda close, Jade struggled to fend off two soldiers with just her quarterstaff. Brynn crawled through a gap and darted behind the soldiers, his little dagger wreaking havoc in unexpected and painful places. Marcus lingered, watching, protecting their backs as more soldiers realised their quarry were escaping.

"Jade!" Phoenix called. "Get Truda and Brynn through the gate. We'll be right behind you."

She grabbed Truda's hand and pulled the girl through a gap created when Brynn hamstrung a soldier. A swift strike with her staff despatched yet another man who attempted to grab the young redheaded girl.

Phoenix dodged a badly-aimed thrust and slipped inside the soldier's guard to slide his blade neatly between exposed ribs. The portal rippled as first Truda then Brynn vanished through it. Jade paused, looking back at them.

"Come on you two. Hurry!" she yelled. "There are more coming. You can't fight them all." She leapt through with one last, anxious look over her shoulder.

Phoenix cast one quick look at Zhudai's men. They were still too far away even for a suicide mission. As much as it galled him, he had to run for it with the others. Phoenix caught Marcus's eye and together they retreated toward the portal, still exchanging blows with Romans as they moved. They were less than five metres away; three, two.

"Go," Phoenix said curtly.

The doorway was too narrow for two people to jump through abreast.

Marcus hesitated then threw himself into the silvery

surface and vanished.

Phoenix deflected a blow aimed at his head and another that would have gutted him. The press of soldiers forced him back. If he went through now and the portal stayed open, how the heck was he going to stop them coming through after him?

The Romans stopped. They formed a loose semicircle in front of him, eyeing the portal with superstitious misgivings. Phoenix grinned. It seemed their fear of Brittonic magic was greater than their desire to capture him. Behind them, he caught a glimpse of Agricola's scarlet cloak billowing as the Governor stalked back toward the portal. His expression was that of apoplectic fury. Apparently the flash-bomb hadn't done any lasting damage.

Swearing, Phoenix tucked his sword under one arm and snatched a pilum from the lax hand of a dead Roman. Hefting it, he took aim and hurled it with all his considerable strength toward the Governor of Brittania. The soldiers around him turned to follow its path, groaning as they saw its trajectory. The spear arced gracefully through the smoky air, sliding down a smooth curve toward its target. Someone shouted a warning. Agricola glanced up a fraction late. He flung himself to one side but the lethal tip sliced through his decorative armour and buried itself in his shoulder. Staggering, he fell backward. Soldiers rushed to his side, hiding him from Phoenix's searching gaze. Had he killed the Governor or only wounded him? He was fairly sure it hadn't been a killing shot, more's the pity.

Whatever the result, it was time to leave - before the soldiers nearest came out of shock and renewed their attack. With a mocking bow, Phoenix turned on his heel. Two swift strides brought him to the doorway. He paused for a moment, wondering whether it would hurt; whether home was on the other side; whether anything was on the other side; whether this was the end of his adventure or just the end of Level One. A large part of him hoped it wasn't over. He'd never felt more alive.

Shrugging, he stepped forward.

There was a sharp sting between his shoulderblades. A rush of agony swept through his chest. He tried to yell but drew only pain into his lungs. Strength fled from his limbs. He fell through the Portal and into blackness.

*****

In his dark prison, Long Baiyu laughed softly. Around his battered body, a faint halo of purple-blue began to shine. His laughter grew until it bounced back to him from the stone walls and rang faintly through the palace above.

The End

Find out more at aikiflinthart.com

Book 1: 80AD - The Jewel of Asgard,   is available now....
Book 2: 80AD - The Hammer of Thor,   is available now....
Book 3: 80AD-The Tekhen of Anuket,   is available now....
Book 4: 80AD - The Sudasharna,   is available now....
Book 5: 80AD - The Yu Dragon,   is available now....

Discover my next series: The Kalima Chronicles here.

A taste of things to come

80AD Level Two

The Hammer of Thor

CHAPTER ONE

Jade opened her eyes to an uneasy world of greys and blacks; of unidentifiable shapes and soft, sighing sounds. She lay on her stomach, awkwardly sprawled on something cold, slippery and hard. Her right knee ached like she'd knocked it and her right hand stung.

"Hello?" Her voice seemed muffled. Something cold and wet feathered across her cheek. She touched her face with numb fingers and shivered. "Phoenix?"

The darkness eased somewhat. Perhaps her eyes were adjusting. Around her patches of light and shadow shifted and swam. It was difficult to tell where the ground ended and the rest of the world began.

She gathered her feet beneath her and staggered upright. Shaking, she pulled the hood of her cloak up and tucked half-frozen fingers into her armpits to warm them. Her backpack slipped off her shoulder, dragging at her arm. As she took an uncertain step, her foot kicked something long and wooden: her quarterstaff. Snatching it up, she tried to feel more secure.

Was she alone here? Wherever this was, it certainly wasn't home. She tried to hold back a rising sense of betrayal. She'd been so certain that finishing Level One would catapult her home again. It hadn't. This wasn't her England. In fact, it probably wasn't England at all.

A wolf howled: distant; mournful; eerie.

Definitely not England.

Sharp, fitful breezes stung her eyes. Jade blinked and

scrubbed a hand over her face, trying to hold back bitter tears of disappointment. She just wanted to go home.

For the hundredth time in the last five days, she wished she'd never turned her father's computer on; never been drawn into this bizarre digital world; wished that she was home again in her warm house with her six annoying sisters. She missed her father; her own, warm, comfortable bed - and hot showers!

Roaming the 80AD world sounded awesome - when she was watching her avatar on a flat screen from the comfort of her father's study. Living it was a whole different thing. Her scared thirteen year old mind was trapped inside the digital body and memories of a seventeen year old half-elf in a strange time and place. She'd been nuts to think living the adventures she'd always read about in books would be romantic and exciting. Right now, the most awesome thing she could think of to see would be the giant golden arches of a MacDonalds restaurant - or her very own bathroom.

The ground crunched as she stamped her feet to warm them. More cold, fluffy stuff fell on her face and Jade at last realised what it was: snow. A wolf howled again, closer; a primeval sound that echoed strangely and made the hairs on the back of her neck rise up. Dark forms around her resolved into trees. She was in a snowy, dark forest somewhere. Well, that didn't help much. How could it be snowing at night when it had been a clear spring dawn in the ancient Britain they had just left?

The last thing she remembered was jumping through the portal from Stonehenge in a desperate attempt to escape a horde of Roman soldiers and their ambitious governor, Agricola. She'd thought the portal was going to get her home but it must have brought her to Level Two of the game, instead. If that was right then home was still a long way off – four more Levels, in fact.

So, if she was on Level Two, where were Phoenix and

the others?

A low moan to her left sent her in that direction, feeling her way carefully. A dark lump in the snow moaned again. Her hands touched leather and steel.

"Phoenix?"

He moaned again.

"Phoenix!"

She dropped to her knees. He lay face down in the snow, his skin cold, pulse a bare thread. She ran her hands over him, using her Spellweaver skills to try and sense injuries. He had fought the Romans until the last to give the rest a chance to get through the portal. Had he been wounded?

Her seeking fingers touched wood. She gasped. Two arrows protruded from his back, very close to his heart by the feel of them. Her instinct was to yank them out but she took her hand away. She had fought the Romans with as much magic as she could. If she pulled them out now, she didn't have the strength to Heal such deep wounds quickly. He would die. His only chance was if they could find shelter and warmth. She needed food and her herbs to replenish enough strength to save him.

She needed help. Where were the others?

"Oh, my head!" A voice behind made her turn.

"Marcus!" She hurried over, slipping in the deepening snow. Strong hands grasped hers. Jade sobbed in relief, clutching at them like a lifeline. "Are you ok?"

"Yes - just a headache bad enough to kill a god. Where are we?" The Roman boy sounded pained.

Another, smaller figure joined them. "Somewhere dark, wet and way too cold," it said, helpfully.

"Brynn!" She hugged him, feeling how thin and small he was beneath his patched clothes. "Where's Truda?"

"I'm here," the young redheaded girl piped up. "It's awful cold here."

She wrapped her too-big druid cloak tighter about

herself. A flurry of wind and snow snatched the hood off her face. In the gloom, her big blue eyes were dark holes in a white oval.

Jade grabbed Marcus's hand and hauled him upright. "Phoenix has been hurt. We need to find shelter or he's going to die."

"Show me," Marcus ordered.

She led them to their fallen friend. Marcus felt his pulse for a long moment.

He shook his head, barely visible in the dim light. "It's too late, Jade. His heart has stopped. He's gone. Phoenix is dead."

TO BE CONTINUED......

....

APPENDIX

ROME:

The Roman Republic (510BC-44BC) sent Julius Caesar in 55BC to investigate Britain. Rome wanted good farming land to grow food crops to support its large population. The Republic transformed into the Roman Empire (44BC to 479AD) shortly after when Julius Caesar declared himself perpetual dictator. It was not until 43AD that Rome created permanent settlements in Britain: when Emperor Claudius sent an army of 40,000 men to overcome the natives. It took several governors many decades to subdue the fierce native tribespeople. Eventually, most submitted but the Picts (the native tribes living in what is now Scotland) did not.

Between 378AD and 410AD, with the economic and military collapse of the Roman Empire, troops and governors were withdrawn from Britain, leaving the country unprotected. It lapsed into petty kingdoms and internal conflict. Soon after, the Viking invasions began and Britain lost much of its Roman culture and "civilisation".

A Roman Governor in a Province such as Brittanica would have had 5 'lictors' (bodyguards) and several 'comites' – companions to act as advisors. The Governor was in charge of collecting taxes for Rome, running military campaigns and dispensing justice as he saw fit.

Roman army:

Contubernium: (tent group) consisted of 8 men

Centuria: (century) was made up of 10 contubernium with a total of 80 men commanded by a centurion (officer)

Cohorts: (cohort) included 6 centuriae or a total of 480 fighting men, not including officers.

Legio: (Legion) consisted of 10 cohorts.

Additionally each Legion had a 120 man Alae (cavalry unit) called the Eques Legionis permanently attached to it possibly to be used as scouts and messengers.

Therefore the total fighting strength of a Legion is: The First Cohort totalling 800 men (5 double-strength centuries with 160 men each); 9 Cohorts (with 6 centuries at 80 men each) for a total 4,320, and an additional 120 man cavalry for a grand total of 5,240 men not including all the officers.

http://www.unrv.com/military/legion.php

Roman measurements:
1 League (Leuga) = 2.22km
1 Mile (milliarium) = 1.48km

Gnaeus Julius Agricola (July 13, 40AD - August 23, 93AD) was the Roman general responsible for much of the Roman conquest of Britain. Arriving in Britain mid-summer of 78AD, Agricola immediately moved against the Ordovices (native tribes of north Wales) and defeated them. He then moved north to the island of Mona (Anglesey), and forced its inhabitants to sue for peace. He established a good reputation as an administrator as well as a commander by reforming the widely corrupt corn tax. He introduced Romanising measures, encouraging communities to build towns on the Roman model and educating the sons of the native nobility in the Roman manner. He also expanded Roman rule north into Caledonia (modern Scotland). He was eventually recalled to Rome in 85AD and died in 93AD.

He had two sons, both of whom died in infancy; plus a daughter who married Tacitus. Tacitus is famous for his written records of Agricola's life and it is from these writings that we get most of our information about Agricola.

BRITAIN

Before the invasion of Britain by the Romans, the islands were inhabited by native Celtic-culture and Brythonic tribes. They lived in iron age fashion, with timber or earthen-walled, thatched "round-houses", basic pottery and agricultural skills. They were farmers living in small village groups, each looking to their own chieftain for guidance. When invaded, however, they proved to be fierce warriors.

Cunetio

The village of Cunetio was originally farmland around the area now called Mildenhall in Wiltshire, UK. When the Romans pushed into the area, a small settlement sprang up around a major crossroads. In later years, the settlement grew into a town with a large stone wall. After the Romans left in about 450AD, it fell into ruin and was lost. In 1978 a hoard of 55000 small-value Roman coins was found there by archaeologists. Recently, the Time Team TV show re-investigated the area and mapped it more thoroughly.

Druids

Little is known of the druids' true functions and beliefs in pre-Roman Britain. It is thought that they served as priests of a sort and held rituals at sacred sites throughout the year that were connected with the Earth Goddess image and various other minor pagan gods and goddesses revered at the time. They were also responsible for upholding laws, settling disputes and teaching students the ideas of astronomy and science of the time.

Language:

The unusual words Brynn and the others occasionally use are from the Ancient Breton language that was spoken by the tribespeople of the time. There are also Welsh words, as Welsh is the closest living relative to the language of the ancient Breton people to whom Brynn belongs.

The words are translated as follows:

Carega Amgarn (Stone Circle - Welsh):
y Twlwyth Teg (The fair people – Welsh):
Plowonida (Wide river – Bretonic):
Leidyr (thief – Welsh):
Hyllion Bagia ('all I bag' – Welsh):
Aurfanon (Welsh – Gold Queen)

THE END

Discover other titles by Aiki Flinthart at:
www.aikiflinthart.com

The 80AD series
(YA Adventure/Fantasy)

80AD Book 1: *The Jewel of Asgard*
80AD Book 2: *The Hammer of Thor*
80AD Book 3: *The Tekhen of Anuket*
80AD Book 4: *The Sudarshana*
80AD Book 5: *The Yu Dragon*

The Kalima Chronicles
(YA Adventure/Fantasy)

IRON (Book 1)

ABOUT THE AUTHOR

Aiki Flinthart lives in Australia. In between running a business and being with her husband of many years, she pursues writing, archery, knife-throwing, martial arts, art, music, bellydancing and watches too much television. After many years of writing for her own amusement, she finally decided to write for others' – and discovered it was even more fun.

Discover other titles by Aiki Flinthart at:
www.aikiflinthart.com

Connect with Aiki on Facebook